Angela's Truth

a novel by

S. M. Dougan

http://www.angelastruth.com

BookSurge, LLC
http://www.booksurge.com

Angela's Truth is a work of fiction. The incidents, names, places and characters are the product of the author's imagination and any resemblance to actual persons, living or dead, businesses, locations or events are completely coincidental.

Cover design by Claire Down

ISBN: 0-9739385-0-1

To order additional copies, please contact us
BookSurge, LLC
www.booksurge.com
1-866-308-6235
orders@booksurge.com

Printed in the U.S.A.

10 9 8 7 6 5 4 3 2 1

This book is dedicated to my son,
Shamus

Yes, you can.

Life is precious. Every day is a blessing. Whether by the careful design of some gracious god, or by simple chance, here we are to see and experience it all. For eons the sun has risen and set. Millennia of days have played out their seemingly random events. With each sunrise comes a new chance, a new beginning - all the days before only stepping stones to this time and place.

A mother holds her new born close to her breast and dreams of the possibilities. She will guide, protect, shelter, and nurture this child until it has grown enough to make its own way. Choices are made and their consequences dealt with. In the end the light dims and fades. The in-between is the legacy; the memory; the sum; the fuel for judgment.

1

Today was one of those days - not a cloud in the sky, a day sweet and pure. The air was warm and fresh; sea birds glided by on wing. Could there be a more beautiful place on earth? So many days had come and gone. So many hopes and dreams fulfilled - so many not.

Elaine pulled herself back to the present. She was aware of what her daughter was saying and the words fueled her own thoughts. "My little girl is so grown up. Twenty years, and now she is going to be married."

From across the table, Angela focused on her mother's eyes. She was annoyed that her Mother did not appear to be paying attention to what she was saying. She had worked hard on this speech. It was intended to convince her mother to aid her in the quest. She now wondered if she was going to have to repeat the whole thing. "Mother, are you listening to me?"

"Sorry dear," her mother replied, shaking her head and smiling, "Yes, I have been listening. I have heard every word and understand completely."

The years of managing her business had made Elaine strong and sure. They had also strengthened not only her ability to hear the spoken word but, more importantly, to understand what was really being said. She noted once again the similarities between motherhood and business management and believed the skills learned in one were almost interchangeable with the other.

The years had been kind to Elaine. Now in her fifties, there were only hints of grey in her hair and a few subtle character wrinkles on her face. She carried herself proudly, exuding confidence, her inner strength evident. Her very presence had the ability to calm those around her.

Elaine smiled sweetly at her daughter. "I was just thinking how proud of you I am. How proud your father would have been." She hesitated, "You won't be able to find him, you know. They keep that information confidential."

Elaine took another bite of her lunch, using this theatrical pause for effect. "Your father and I knew that when we decided to go ahead with the process. All donors are kept confidential. Your father and I wanted a child - you - so badly but we couldn't do it on our own. We made the choice only after a great deal of careful consideration." She paused again. She wanted to give weight to every sentence. "The man, whoever he was, was a sample in a test tube, a donor - nothing more."

Elaine was deliberately trying to make the sperm donor sound insignificant. She wanted to downplay any influence he might have in their lives. She wanted the thought of him to be of as little importance to Angela as a subtle change in the direction of the wind. She took another sip of her wine, fully aware of just how incredibly significant he really was. Without him her daughter simply wouldn't exist. However, the road Angela was proposing to travel would only cause her pain. It was folly, and Elaine couldn't stand the thought of the hurt this pursuit could cause her daughter.

Elaine returned her gaze to Angela and forced her voice to be calm and quiet, "Please, Angela, let it go. You're getting married soon. That's all that should be on your mind right now. You're building your life. Please, leave the past in the past where it belongs."

Angela had chosen a spring wedding more for its symbolism than anything else. She believed that spring was the time of new beginnings. All the hope and promise of new life lay ahead - new promise, new hope, and life reborn.

Philip was a dozen years older than Angela. Elaine had expressed concern about this age difference on many occasions, feeling it would eventually come between them. She felt Angela was only just beginning to experience life while Philip was well on his way. However, Angela simply didn't see it that way. She was confident of his love for her. Her love for him was equally genuine and complete. She saw herself with him in complete happiness for the rest of her life. That was the only thing that mattered. Whatever life threw at her, as long as there was that special someone beside her, she knew anything could be overcome.

Angela was sitting with her hands cupped in front of her face, her elbows resting squarely on the table. She was frustrated at not being able to convince her mother to help her. She had no idea how deeply her mother really felt, nor how much she really wanted to know about him also. Elaine pointed at her daughter with her fork, "Finish your lunch. I have to get back to the office."

Angela looked down at her half eaten meal and pushed it aside. "I'm not really hungry," she said and took a sip of her wine instead. She glanced aimlessly around the restaurant. The place was filled with happy couples and families enjoying the afternoon and she wondered about their stories. Her gaze wandered off shore. A small sailboat was doing its dance in harmony with the rise and fall of the sea. Angela recalled the many lunches she and her mother had enjoyed in this spot, at this table. The fresh sea air and the sweet caress of the warm ocean breeze added a special flavor to these times. Life is so precious, so precious, she thought, "But… who am I?"

Angela's eyes returned to her mother, "You're right of course, Mom." She knew that once her mother had shut the door, that door was shut. There was no point pursuing this conversation any further. "I'm sure he is married, with grown children. He has a life out there somewhere. Why should I complicate things for him? He shot into a sample cup, picked up a few bucks, and here I am."

Elaine hid her shock at such a cold remark coming from her daughter. She was now certain that her daughter was set on her course. Angela had to know, but Elaine knew she couldn't support her in this pursuit. Angela would have to find her own way, and learn for herself the futility of her desire. She would have to experience the pain of failure on her own. Elaine felt sorrow for the pain her sweet child would soon experience.

"Would you like to ride back with me, dear?" Elaine asked as she handed her credit card to the waiter.

"No thanks, Mom. I have some things to do in town. I'll see you at home later?" Angela knew the name of the clinic. Today was the day.

"Yes dear. I should be home around seven."

Angela smiled warmly at her mother as she got up to leave. Elaine gently but firmly clutched her daughter's hand. She had one last chance, "Sweetheart, I love you more than life itself, you know that. Trust me on this. I know you very well. Let this go. No good can come of it. Your Dad, God rest his soul, and I are your parents. We are your mother and father. We are your family."

Angela looked down at her mother and saw the pain in her eyes. She smiled sweetly and covered her mother's hand with her own. "I know. I love you too, Mom. It ends here." Angela's voice was gentle, calm, almost convincing. Her training in sales - make the prospect believe - came through. Her mother had taught her well. Angela left the restaurant thinking how much she hated lying to her mother.

Elaine hadn't been convinced. As she sat alone at the table her mind wandered back to a time long ago when life was so different. Everything was in front of her then. She had been so happy, so full of hope, so full of youthful exuberance. She had had no cares in the world.

He hadn't been anyone special to her. Just a man serving drinks in the campus pub. Like so many others at the time, he was working to put himself through business school. She had seen him elsewhere on campus, even in some of her own classes. He was, however, just a name and a face. She had thought him attractive, but that was all.

The first time he saw her, the story was somewhat different. He fell deeply in love with her at that first glance. He had known immediately that he would love her for the rest of his life. He was also painfully aware that she didn't know he existed. He would change that.

It had taken him a little time to work up the courage to make his first move but once started, he pursued her relentlessly. It had become almost an obsession for him. Eventually, she allowed him the privilege of her company for a single night out. That was all he needed - the relationship grew to the inevitable sacred union before their God.

Things had been so uncomplicated then. They had lived simply, working side by side, developing a business to support themselves. They had nurtured the business as if it was a living being and it fulfilled all their monetary and many of their spiritual needs. Under their careful guidance, the business grew and prospered, and along with it, their love for each other.

In time, as they became more comfortable and secure, they decided they needed a child to share their lives. The topic had been discussed with more and more frequency until it became an obsession. Unsure if it was personal will or age old instinct, they knew they must have a child.

While their efforts to achieve their goal were enjoyable, they remained unsuccessful. After many tests and much emotional upheaval, they decided to seek outside help. Many options were available but, because of the confidentiality, the decision was made to use a nameless sperm donor. The process was involved, almost surreal, but successful and, in time, a beautiful baby girl arrived in their lives.

He had been totally absorbed with his new little girl and could hardly believe the depth of love he could feel for another. His desire to make everything perfect for her drove him until he was almost crazed. In the end, his hopes and dreams were stolen from him by his own body; his heart gave out.

Elaine remembered how she had laid him to his final rest, in the dirt and alone. She had stood by his grave with their young daughter at her side. The two looked at the cold wood and earth and Elaine thought of all the things that would never be. Their little angel was devastated. "Where had her daddy gone? Why did he leave her? What had she done?"

Elaine decided on that day that, even though the world would be cruel, Angela would always know the truth – she would see to that. It was then Elaine made the decision to devote her life to this little girl. Everything she would be, everything she would do, would be for Angela. She was the only thing in life that mattered now.

Elaine's mind reluctantly returned to the present. She realized her memories seemed jaded and disjointed, as if they were a tale relayed to her by someone else. However, even though she wanted to forget and leave the past in the past where it belonged, she knew the story was hers. It was time to go back to work. As she left the restaurant, she thought of her daughter and her fiancé. Will he be good to her? Will he always love and protect her? She knew she would always be there for them. It was her duty.

* * * * *

Philip hung up the phone, looked around his office and smiled. He loved the power he possessed. He had told his decorators that the office needed to demonstrate his power and his success - he was pleased with the job they had done for him. The walls were paneled in mahogany. Bookshelves with leaded glass doors lined one wall. The room was filled with exquisite pieces of art and literature. Many of the books were his; he had read them many times. The other impressive titles were purchased simply to fill the remaining space. He had never read those, and had no intention of doing so. The art chosen for him was unique. On the walls hung original oil paintings by well known artists, but again, he didn't buy any of it. He didn't have an opinion on those pieces. To his friends, he referred to them as his pictures.

On one side of the office was an arrangement of four couches surrounding an oversized coffee table. He used that part of the office to entertain and to conduct informal meetings. All the formal meetings were held in the boardroom down the hall.

His desk, an ornate hand carved mahogany and dark walnut piece, had been custom made for him by an old world craftsman. It was stunning. It was the only piece in the whole room that he had specified himself, and was the only piece he really loved. It housed his computer, telephone, a writing area, a Tiffany desk lamp, and a few personal pieces including a beautiful photograph of Angela in an elaborate gold frame. The whole office had been set up to impress and intimidate, and it made him feel important.

In reality, he was very much a "down to basics" kind of a guy. He was just as at home sitting by a campfire as he was sitting as chairman in the boardroom. Of the two, he preferred the campfire.

However, he believed the façade was necessary for the business he had built from the ground up. He had often considered business to be like war – every day a new battle must be fought and won. He always felt it was him against them and he knew he had to win, at any cost.

Of late, the numbers were out of line and profits were down; he had to cut back. With one telephone call fifty people were out of work. He fully appreciated the significance of what he had done and was aware of the impact on the displaced employees and their families. It was not a decision he made lightly but when all the data was analyzed, he had no other choice. It was the only thing he could do. Once he had made the decision, he didn't have any trouble doing the deed. He didn't feel any emotional involvement; he really didn't care one way or the other.

The buzzer on the phone disturbed his thoughts. He picked it up, "Yes, Melody?"

Melody's voice sounded as sweet as her name, "Mr. Maxwell from the Child Development Center is here. He would like to see you, if you can spare ten minutes."

Philip thought to himself, "What the hell does he want? The presentation is in thirty minutes. Can't it wait 'til then?", then he spoke into the phone, his voice was masked pleasantness, "Certainly, I always have time for him."

Philip hung up the phone, annoyed. He got up and started walking to the door which opened as Melody escorted a sheepish Mr. Maxwell into the office.

Philip's smile was pleasant as he greeted Mr. Maxwell, thinking, "This guy could really stand to lose a couple hundred pounds. What a pig."

Philip offered his hand, "Mr. Maxwell, nice to see you as usual. Would you like a coffee?" asked Philip, gesturing to the couch area.

Mr. Maxwell shook his head, obviously nervous at being in Philip's office. "Thank you. No. I don't want to take up too much of your time."

Philip smiled at him then dismissed Melody with a nod. She closed the door and Philip sat on the couch across from Mr. Maxwell, his smile fixed. "So, what can I do for you, Mr. Maxwell?"

Mr. Maxwell cleared his throat nervously before he spoke. "Mr. Evans, as you are aware, I'm the Chairman of the Board for the Center. I just wanted to thank you in person before the presentation. Your contribution to the Center is so very generous, I can't thank you enough. I can assure you the money will be well spent. It will do much good."

Philip thought to himself, cynically, "Yeah, yeah. Whatever."

His jaw started to feel the twinge of the forced smile as he responded, "Not at all, Mr. Maxwell. It's the least I can do. I always like to help. You people do such good work. I've been very fortunate and I just wanted to give something back."

Mr. Maxwell nodded as if he understood what Philip was all about, "It was such a nice idea to hold the press conference for the presentation. It will give the Center much needed exposure. Hopefully more people like you will come forward to help."

Philip smiled at that, "I certainly hope so. That's why I thought we should do it this way."

Philip had notified the Center a few days earlier telling them that he wanted to make the contribution and that it would be in the form of a personal cheque. He had thought it would look better than if it had simply been another corporate sponsorship. It had been Philip's idea that they make a presentation of a Certificate of

Appreciation to him. It was his idea that they do the presentation in front of the media, and he had assured them that the amount of his contribution would be substantial enough to get the media's attention. He had convinced the Center that it would be great publicity for them and that he would like to help them in anyway he could. He had been very convincing. He could see himself making the exchange in front of the cameras and knew he would look good.

Philip continued, pleasantly, "Was there anything else, Mr. Maxwell?"

Mr. Maxwell got up as if on cue and smiled at Philip, "No. Thank you. That was all. I just wanted to thank you personally." He reached out his hand to Philip.

Philip took it, "It was a pleasure as always, Mr. Maxwell. I'll see you downstairs in a few minutes?"

Mr. Maxwell nodded politely as he headed for the door. Philip watched him leave. It hadn't been necessary for this man to come and see him personally. It was, after all, only money. However, Philip did feel good that the money was going to be appreciated and useful, although that was merely an ancillary benefit. The publicity he was going to receive from his donation was the truly important factor. The value of publicity was far more than just the amount of the cheque.

He had never actually been to the Center, nor did he know what they did there, and frankly, he didn't care. Many people were going to see him make the presentation and, as a result, he was going to look good and, therefore, so would the business.

* * * * *

As is typical in most major cities, parking downtown can be a challenge, so Angela was thrilled to find a parking lot next to the clinic. She pulled into the first vacant stall and directly in front of her car was a large sign, "Show your parking receipt to the receptionist for validation". She smiled to herself, "Is that all it takes?"

She entered the building through the double glass doors. The receptionist was fumbling with some papers at the counter in front of her. Angela approached the uniformed young woman and smiled. Printed on the tag pinned to the front of her uniform was her name, "Jane Z.". Jane looked up and smiled, "Good afternoon. May I help you?"

Angela continued to smile, placed her hands on the counter, and using her best innocent expression replied, "I hope so. I'm looking for some information."

"Certainly," and with that Jane sat down in front of her computer and struck a few keys. Defiant at her attempts, the screen stayed blank. She muttered under her breath, "Damn thing."

Angela glanced at the blank screen and then back at Jane and smiled again at her obvious frustration. Jane looked back at her and smiled, realizing the impression she was giving was somewhat less than professional. "OOPS! Sorry about that. These darn computers have been down all day." She gestured with her thumb to some obscure place behind her, "The tech is in the back working on our systems. He was supposed to be finished before we opened this morning." Her eye caught the clock on the wall, "Two thirty! Two thirty and he's still not finished!" She looked back at Angela and smiled, "Sorry," and chuckled nervously, "You really don't care, do you? Please have a seat," pointing to the lounge area.

"I'll see if one of our counselors can see you. Is this your first visit?"

"Yes, first time," Angela replied and turned to the lounge thinking, "She thinks I'm a client. Well that's probably good - it will at least get me inside."

Angela sat in the closest chair in the empty lounge area. "Comfortable," was her first impression as she began to examine the individual elements that made up the decor. It was obvious the planning of the room had been given careful consideration. Clearly, the space was meant to look and feel comfortable and relaxing. There was not a hint of the clinical atmosphere one might expect at such a place. The walls were painted in a soft pastel and hung with tasteful original oil paintings. She considered each piece for a moment, and then glanced to the next, and then the next. She didn't recognize the artists' names, but the work was pleasant enough.

Each piece of furniture, as well, was equal to the rest of the surroundings. She concluded that the decorating was certainly good enough to be in someone's home never mind the waiting area of a clinic. She was impressed. Undoubtedly, that had been the whole idea. Make your clients comfortable, and they will be more relaxed. "Make the prospect believe". She took a magazine from the pile on the table and started to leaf through it. She had no idea what the magazine was nor did she care. A waiting room is just a waiting and waiting wasn't something she wanted to do. She had waited long enough already.

Within minutes a pleasant looking blonde woman walked into the lounge. She was a few years older than Angela and about the same height. She walked confidently towards Angela, offering her hand. "Hi. I'm Gina, how do you do?"

Angela smiled as she shook the other's hand and thought, "The receptionist forgot to get my name", then spoke politely, "I'm Angela Michails. I'm fine. Thank you." Angela had noticed that Gina didn't introduce herself as Doctor - she had simply said "Gina".

"Glad to meet you, Ms. Michails. Please, come inside and let's see what we can do for you."

Angela unceremoniously tossed the magazine back to the pile as she got up, "Please, call me Angela. Ms. Michails sounds like my mother," they chuckled politely.

"Of course, Angela, I do have to apologize, though. Things are a bit hectic around here today," Gina's voice sounded genuine as they continued into her office.

"Yes." Angela replied as she sat in front of Gina's desk. "Jane was mentioning something about work on your systems?" she masked her lack of interest expertly.

"Yes. The system is only three months old and now it has crashed or something. As you can probably imagine, it has really made a mess of things around here." Gina shook her hands in front of her as if to clear the air and pointed to the side wall indicating the technician was working on the other side. "Well, anyway, he should be finished soon. Things can get back to normal - hopefully. We have no idea as yet how much damage has been done. Thankfully, it hasn't been too busy here today or we would really be in a pickle!"

Gina was unaware that the computer technician could hear everything she was saying. The building designers hadn't been concerned with noise transmission between Gina's office and the next room. They knew that room would only be used to house the computer system and were more interested in keeping building costs down than they were about sound insulation.

The computer technician looked up from his terminal, glancing at the shared wall. He had heard virtually everything said in Gina's office all day - everything that she had discussed with her clients as well as what she had been saying about him. His displeasure with her was growing and he muttered under his breath, "I'm going as fast as I can."

Gina opened a fresh file folder and started making notes on the form it contained. "Okay Angela. What can I do for you? My receptionist tells me you would like some information on the insemination process? You are obviously looking to have a child?"

Angela squirmed nervously in her chair, thinking, "Here goes".

"Yes." she said out loud, and thought, "But not today!"

Angela chose her tone carefully as she continued, "I noticed that you didn't introduce yourself as doctor."

She was genuinely curious about Gina's credentials but didn't want to appear intimidating or annoying.

Noting Angela's tone, Gina looked up from the folder and smiled, "Of course, Angela. Forgive me. I'm not a doctor. I'm a counselor and the clinic manager. The clinic has retained the services of a very well respected physician who takes care of the actual procedures and all the medical details. She is very good. I assure you this is a very legitimate facility. The clinic has been doing this for some twenty two years now. We adhere to a very strict set of guidelines for ethical standards of conduct and we maintain absolute confidentiality."

Those words hit Angela like a hammer, "Standards of conduct", "Absolute confidentiality". They were important words to most people, but they weren't the words Angela wanted to hear. The technician behind the wall looked up when he heard Gina's comments and chuckled, "You have no bloody idea, lady" and returned to his work.

Angela smiled, "What kind of information do you have on the donors that come to your clinic? What's the screening process?"

Angela knew she needed to establish trust, and somehow build rapport with Gina. These questions were intended to help achieve that goal. Angela knew that was the only way she would be able to get the information she so desperately wanted. She was now wondering whether or not she would ever learn who her father was.

Gina responded to Angela's questions quickly. "Well, we start by having each donor complete a questionnaire which we keep on permanent file." She pointed at the wall again, "The potential donor then signs a series of releases that enable us to perform certain medical examinations and to obtain his medical records. We are very thorough." There was pride in her voice. "We compile a summary of our findings and if the donor is considered suitable, samples are taken and stored carefully within the facility. You would be shown a catalog of sorts which lists the donors by general physical attributes; hair and eye color, ethnic background - things of that nature. You would then choose a donor. Our physician has been involved throughout the whole process - she is the one who will actually accept the donor and perform the procedure when the time comes. You will have a series of examinations yourself. We want to be as sure as we can that the procedure will have every reasonable chance of success."

Gina paused to gather her thoughts, "You do have to realize, though, that there are no guarantees. I can't emphasize that enough. We do have a very respectable success rate, relatively speaking, but there are still failures. You need to know that up front." She paused to allow sufficient time for that information to be digested before proceeding, "Generally speaking, most of the women who come to us have already been trying to get pregnant. They have been to their own doctors who have indicated that everything is normal. Our exams are really just to confirm the physicians' conclusions. Provided those exams are satisfactory, a number of your eggs will be harvested and fertilized with the donor's sperm in our lab. When we are satisfied that we have a viable sample, the fertilized eggs are returned to you. From that point on things are pretty much in Mother Nature's hands."

Angela was genuinely stunned, "How cold... how sterile and utterly nameless". Gina sensed Angela's discomfort and quickly changed from her analytical tone to that of a caring friend. "Believe me, Angela, when we have finished, everything goes as God intended. In nine months chances are pretty good you will have your beautiful baby." Gina completed her obligatory speech and now wanted to put Angela at ease. "Tell me about yourself. What do you do?"

Angela refocused on the reason for her being in this office, "I'm a sales rep. for my mother's firm."

Gina nodded approvingly, "A family business. How nice that must be for you. You said your mother's firm, what does your dad do?"

Angela appeared a little distant before she collected herself, "He died when I was five."

"Oh, I'm sorry," Gina responded sincerely as she made a few notes in the file.

Angela waved it off, "No, really, it was a long time ago."

Gina paused for what she believed an appropriate amount of time then continued, "And how long have you been married?"

"Well actually," Angela stops and thinks, "Careful." then continues, "Actually I'm not married. I'm engaged. We're going to be married in a couple of weeks."

Gina didn't hide her surprise as she looked up from the file, "Ah, congratulations. Sorry, why are you here? Does your fiancé already know there may be a problem?"

Angela was feeling the pressure of her deepening lie as she responded, "We're not sure. We think there might be a problem. We don't know. I'm just looking for some information on the processes and procedures." Then she thought, "This charade is getting me nowhere, except deeper. I should just come clean and hope for the best." Angela took a deep breath as she continued looking innocently at Gina, "The truth is, Gina, I'm not exactly a prospective client."

Gina straightened up in her chair, visibly annoyed as she looked directly at Angela, "Then may I ask, what, exactly, are you doing here?"

"Everything I have told you is true," Angela started, hoping to make a plea to Gina's femininity.

"My mother was a client of this clinic, I am the result." She paused a second to let that sink in, "With my wedding coming up and my Dad no longer with us." She paused again, thinking, "This isn't going well". Then continued, "Look, I really just want to find out who my biological father is. I'd like to know who I am before I become someone else, if you know what I mean. I'd like to think he would want to see me get married. I just know that I really need to meet him. I need to know who I am." Angela was almost begging now.

"Touching Miss Michails, really." Gina was clearly not amused. "Our records are confidential. The anonymity of our donors is guaranteed." Gina sounded like a replay of some bad recording. "Your mother must have told you that. Did you honestly think you could just waltz in here, weave some tale, and I would open our records to you?"

Angela was painfully aware that her original plan had been flawed, and the backup plan wasn't going to work either, "Gina, please. Put yourself in my shoes. I am who I am as a result of my biological parents, yet I have no idea who my father is. I barely knew my Dad. My only memories are those I have created from the stories my mother has told me. She has been my only family for the last 15 years. Wouldn't you want to know? Don't you care? Are you really that heartless?" Tears starting flowing from Angela's eyes and ran down her rouged cheeks. They were real and she fought to hold them back.

Gina's mood softened and she leaned forward on her desk, "Miss Michails", she shook her head, "Angela, I'm not heartless, really. I sympathize with you. Really I do. But our guidelines are set up for good reason. There are a lot of people out there that really want a family - good people, like your own parents. They have the means to provide a good home for a child, but for reasons, haven't been able to have one. There are many options available to them. This is just one of them. People choose this option precisely because of the anonymity, and to develop the special bond that can only come from the actual bearing of a child. For all intents and purposes the child is really theirs. If we divulged donors' names and such - well let's just say there could be all kinds of unpleasant ramifications. Would the donor be financially responsible to the child? What happens if the parents die, would he be responsible for the child? If our gentlemen knew there was a possibility of these types of situations, how many do you think would be interested in being donors? Not many, I would imagine. No donors, then those people wouldn't have this type of child rearing experience. You wouldn't exist. That's why our donors are kept anonymous. It is very important to some people, including your own parents." She pauses for a minute, reflecting, "Like me."

Angela was caught off guard by that comment, "Like you?"

"Yes, I'm a client as you put it. My husband was injured on the job before we could have a child. We decided that this was the best way for us." Gina smiled, obviously pleased, "We have a beautiful little boy. It was the whole process and the birth of our baby that convinced me to come and work here. I really wanted to help other people."

Angela had noticed the family picture on Gina's desk - a happy family all together, and smiling. Angela recognized it as something missing from her own life.

The computer technician was busily working at his terminal and had heard the whole conversation. He hadn't noticed sympathetic tears welling up in his eyes but when he did, he chuckled and shook it off, "You sap!"

"So, Angela, believe me. I know what you are talking about." Gina continued, "But it changes nothing."

Angela composed herself, "What are you going to say to your son when he asks who his biological father is? Believe me, that day will come."

Gina hardened, "That day will never come. Believe me, I have asked myself that very question hundreds of times. My husband and I agree, we will never tell him the truth. It is something he really doesn't need to know. We are his parents and that is that."

Angela was getting angry, "Don't you think your son, or I for that matter, have the right to know who we really are. Who our biological father is? What gene pool we are from - our ancestry? What things we might expect for our own children?"

Gina knew these were all very real arguments. She had wrestled with them many times herself. The parents' rights, the donors' rights, the children's rights. Which perspective is correct? God alone will have to be the judge of that.

"Reality is perception, Miss Michails. You're in sales, you know that." Gina could hardly believe she said those words.

Angela was stunned. "We're not talking about a used car or a better blender or some other such thing. In the name of God are you going to help me or not," Angela had lost all control.

"Thank you for stopping by Miss Michails," Gina closed the file on her desk and hit the buzzer on her phone, "Jane will show you to the door. Good day."

Gina's expression was as empty as was possible in a living person. Angela stopped short of the door and turned as if to try again. She could see tears growing in Gina's eyes and knew it was pointless.

When the office door closed behind Angela, Gina sobbed out loud and dropped her face into her hands. "God, forgive me!" she cried out, praying for absolution.

Almost immediately there was a knock on the office door. She looked up and wiped her face. "Who is it?" she screamed. The door opened and the computer technician was standing there.

"Yes, Dwayne, what is it!?" Gina said, almost disappointed at seeing him.

"Sorry to bother you, Ma'am, but I'm just about finished. I just need to run a couple diagnostics on your terminal. Ah, just to make sure you're up."

"Ah, yeah, sure," she got up and gestured to her chair. "I'll be right back, Dwayne. Do what you have to do. I'm glad you were able to get things fixed." There was virtually no emotion in her voice as she spoke and left the room.

Dwayne smiled insincerely and thought, "Yeah, suffer, you bitch."

Sitting at her desk, Dwayne tapped a few keys. When he was sure Gina was gone, he reached over and opened the file on her desk. "Angela Michails," he read and closed it again. Satisfied with his work, he returned to the computer room to collect his tools. "Another mission accomplished", he said out loud, "Damn, I'm good."

Outside, Angela unlocked the door of her car and got in. Instinctively the key slid into the ignition then both hands found the steering wheel as she slumped forward and began to cry. She knew she would never be able to get into that clinic again, nor would she ever learn her lineage.

Dwayne left the clinic through the back door and saw Angela in her car. He paused for a second looking at her and smiled as he put his tools in his van and left.

2

It was just past 6:30 p.m. and Angela was curled up on the couch with a half finished glass of wine in her hand. She was staring aimlessly at the unlit fireplace and didn't hear her mother's arrival.

"Hello sweetheart. How was your afternoon?" Elaine asked. Angela's mind still focused elsewhere hadn't heard her mother approaching. When Elaine reached Angela, she bent over and kissed her gently on the top of her head.

Angela twitched with a start, "Mom, hi, you're home."

Elaine chuckled quietly, "Sorry, Angela. I didn't mean to startle you. Go on a little trip without leaving the room did you, dear?"

"Sorry Mom. I didn't hear you come in. How was your afternoon?" Angela took a sip of her wine as her focus returned to the room.

Elaine responded as she headed toward the small bar to get herself a glass of wine, "You know. It's the same old, same old." Elaine didn't like to talk about business when she was at home.

Angela glanced over her shoulder and saw her mother's back. She quickly wiped both sides of her face, hoping all signs of the tears were gone.

"What did you do this afternoon, dear?" Elaine asked as she filled her wine glass.

Both Elaine and Angela were fond of a local vintage from an estate winery just down the road, which each year produced quantities of this very pleasant wine. Elaine made a point, year after year, of picking up several cases. When she and her daughter entertained, they bought the popular names for their guests. However, for their private use, this was the only brand that would do.

"Actually, Mom, I did a little shopping. With so much going on right now, I needed a bit of a diversion." Angela didn't lie. Before going to the clinic, she had visited a number of small shops downtown feeling a little recreational shopping would help her relax and prepare. She knew it would take courage to go to the clinic and proceed with her inquiries. Well, she had been to the clinic, she had tried, and she had failed. Her eyes now wore the scars of that attempt.

Elaine returned the crystal decanter to the silver tray as she turned back to her daughter. She nodded her head approvingly. "That was probably a good idea, dear. You should take tomorrow as well. You can soak in a nice tub, and perhaps go for a walk on the beach. I think you could use a serious, 'me' day."

Elaine had taken great pains decorating this part of the house. She had said, "I want this to be the soul room. I want to feel comfortable and relaxed as soon as I walk across the threshold."

The deep red walls joined a pure white ceiling adorned with original plaster artistry in an old world style. The floors were a dark hardwood, most of which was covered with an antique Persian rug that Elaine had purchased at an estate auction. The seating consisted of several overstuffed antiques which complimented the colors of the room exceptionally well. Every piece of furniture, every little knick-knack, every piece of art had been painstakingly chosen for this room, one piece at a time. Once one nestled into a chair, the whole world disappeared or became clearer, depending on one's frame of mind. It had quickly become Angela's favorite room.

Elaine joined Angela on the couch. As she took a sip of her wine she looked into her daughter's eyes. The strains of the day were clearly visible. She could sense what else Angela had tried to do that day but knew better than to ask. She decided that Angela would share that story when she was ready. Instead Elaine asked, "Did you see my future son-in-law today?"

Angela was shocked at herself, she hadn't thought about her fiancé at all. She pulled herself together and chuckled inaudibly, "No, Mom. Philip left on that business trip this afternoon... Remember?"

Elaine gently smacked her forehead with an open hand and laughed politely, "Of course, I knew that. When is he back?" she asked.

"Day after tomorrow, I think." was Angela's matter-of-fact reply.

"That's that then. Tomorrow is your day. You are going to take it easy and just enjoy yourself." Elaine knew what her daughter needed, she always did. She had sensed the day had gone badly and knew the reason was far more personal than Angela had told her. Elaine half hoped that Angela would continue to look for him and would be successful. Elaine wanted to meet him as well. She believed she would probably like him. After all, Angela was the result of both of them and therefore, he must be someone she would like. However, obviously something had not gone well.

Angela took another sip of her wine and looked back toward the fireplace. "Mom, I have way too much to do. The wedding is..."

"Angela, I'm not making a suggestion here. I'm not giving you a choice. You are taking tomorrow. We have hired professionals to do the leg work. You don't need to be involved everyday. Everything for the wedding is going according to plan. The arrangements are precisely the way you wanted them to be. You can take one day to relax." Her mother was a stubborn woman, and in all her life Angela had never known her to be off the mark. Angela smiled, and looked down at her wine, " Yes, Mummy." They both chuckled at that.

Angela looked intently at her mother, "Seriously, Mom. I've been thinking. What are you going to do once I'm married?" Angela looked around the room again. "This house is so big - too big. You shouldn't be here all by yourself." Angela was genuinely concerned. She had been worried about her mother from the day she became engaged to Philip. Angela had wanted to discuss this with her, but never seemed to find exactly the right moment, now was as good a time as any. Besides, Angela needed to focus on something other than her disappointments of the day.

Elaine ran her finger around the rim of her wine glass as she glanced around the room. "I have given this a lot of thought, dear and I agree. This is an awfully big house for just me. Your father built this house for us after we married. It was our first house and we have always lived here. Your whole life has been here. His memory is alive for me here." Elaine paused and shook her head before continuing, "This isn't just a house. It's our home. I can't give it up. I just can't. Besides, I have people to help me keep it up." Elaine had made the decision.

"I've decided to take an apartment in town." Elaine continued, "It will eliminate the commute, but I will keep this house and stay here on the weekends, or any other time I need to."

Angela nodded, and smiled politely at her mother, not sure what to think. Since Angela's father had died, Elaine had thrown herself into the work of managing the company she and her husband had started. She had no interest in any other men. Although there had been many suitors over the years, she had been so totally in love with her husband, she couldn't think of any other man in that way. Now, all these years later, she was still in love with that memory. As far as she was concerned, she was still married.

Elaine put her glass down on the table and got up, "I'm going to get out of these clothes. Have you eaten yet?"

"No. I'm not really hungry." Angela smiled.

"I don't believe that for a second, dear. When I come back down, we'll make some popcorn, put in a sappy movie, and have a good cry." Elaine waved her hand aimlessly through the air, smiling as she left.

Angela looked at her mother as she disappeared up the stairs. The sarcastic tone of her voice was unmistakable, "Sounds good, Mom."

The phone rang, startling Angela. She spun around on the couch and picked up the receiver, "Hello?"

"Hi. Is this Angela Michails?" Angela didn't recognize the man's voice.

Her reply was polite and inquisitive. "Yes, it is. Who is this?"

The man's voice was obviously nervous. "You were at the clinic today. You are trying to find your biological father?"

Angela pushed. "Who is this?"

There was silence on the phone.

"Call me Bill." He paused again for a second or two. Angela chuckled, "This clown has seen too many movies," she thought.

"I have the information you are looking for," Bill continued.

Angela wasn't amused anymore, "Listen, Bill... or whoever the hell you are. This isn't funny. What do you want?"

"I'm not joking," Bill barked. "I'm dead serious. I know what you are looking for. I have it. Are you interested or not?"

Angela pulled herself together and thought, "What if he is for real? Is it possible? Don't blow this."

"Okay, Bill. You have my attention. You're obviously a shrewd business man," she lied, but continued in her best professional voice. "You have something I want and you obviously want something in return. What's the deal?"

With that, she glanced down at the call display and saw the name and phone number of the caller. It wasn't "Bill". She grabbed the pen that lay beside the phone and jotted them both down as she waited for his response.

Bill was surprised by Angela and thought to himself, "Man, this is easy. Damn I'm good. Ask for fifty thousand. Yeah, fifty thousand is a good number."

Bill finally answered, "Twenty thousand dollars." "Damn. I was going to ask for fifty", he thought as soon as he said it, but paused for effect anyway. "Meet me tomorrow, noon. Twenty thousand in hundreds, and your search will be over."

Angela was screaming inside, "You slimy little... You're trading my life for mere money. You are lower than low" She spoke, masking her anger at him. "You want twenty thousand dollars? That's a lot of money. I don't think I can get my hands on that kind of money that soon."

Bill was obviously annoyed at her attempt to barter, "Listen, lady. People like you spend that kind of money on a night on the town." He knew he was exaggerating, but was making a point.

Angela forced herself to be quiet for a few seconds. She wanted him to believe that she was totally captured by him. "You're good, Bill," she chuckled to herself, "It was worth a shot. Okay you win." She couldn't keep it up any longer and her tone changed to that of the desperate person she actually was. "But how do I know you really can deliver what you promise?"

He noticed the change in the timbre of her voice and almost felt sorry for her - almost. "Listen, Angela... Can I call you Angela?" He didn't wait for an answer," I really want to help you. I really do. What's wrong with me making a few bucks for my trouble? I have it all; his name; his address. Hell, I even have access to his dental records, if you want that. This isn't a scam. I'm for real." He paused for a few seconds to think, "I tell you what. I'm going to go out on limb here. Meet me at the bus station. Put the money in a locker. I'll have a bouquet of flowers in my hand. Sit beside me. You can look over the information. When you see it is real, give me the key and our business is done, agreed?"

Angela was cautiously convinced and thought, “Okay, he is a slime ball but there are a few things lower.” She drew in a deep breath, and exhaled slowly as she spoke, "Agreed, tomorrow, noon." She hung up the phone and picked up the piece of paper. She read it to herself several times, and put it in her pocket.

"Who was that, dear?" Elaine startled Angela by her return.

Angela stared at the phone, then at her mother. "Oh, just some creep trying to sell me something."

Elaine shook her head knowingly, "Yeah, those telemarketers don't know the word "No". What an awful way to make a living." She headed off toward the kitchen and called back to Angela, "Did you pick a movie yet?"

Angela's hand was still in her pocket and she felt the paper one more time before pulling her hand out. She looked over at the video stand, "Ah, not yet. I'll grab something."

3

All night Angela's mind had been preoccupied with thoughts of "Bill" and the information he had promised. Thoughts of what the future might hold had prevented her from getting a decent sleep. Noon wasn't coming fast enough for her. Lying in bed, she glanced over at the clock - 8:15 a.m., her mother would have left by now. She wondered briefly if maybe she should have told her mother about the phone call. Perhaps she should have told her mother that today the search would be over. As she got out of bed and went to fill the bath, she decided that it was probably best she hadn't shared that information. "A nice hot soak is what I need," Angela thought. She chuckled remembering what her mother had said the night before, "Soak in a nice tub, and then perhaps go for a walk on the beach." That was exactly what Angela was going to do.

The warmth of the bath water soothed Angela as it surrounded and supported her. The bath was the one place in the world where reality didn't exist; the one place where only selected senses were allowed to exist. It was like being asleep and awake at the same time - no dreams, no thoughts, just the sound of her breathing, and the scent of the perfumed bubbles. The warmth and freedom allowed her to relax and to center herself. It allowed her to prepare her mind for the day that lay ahead.

She had dressed slowly, savoring the lingering hypnotic effects of the bath. Reality returned on the trip to the beach. The world buzzed hurriedly around her as she drove. The mornings were always busy around town, but the beach was usually deserted. Late nights were quiet at the beach as well making them another good time for these walks. Of the two, Angela preferred the mornings.

All around her, she could hear the sounds of the sea and the city in competitive harmony. She could see the sea creatures going about their routines, the birds swooping, and the seals surfacing and diving again. In her minds eye, she could picture the city people busily going about their daily routines as well.

Walking on the beach always took her mind away from the realities of human life, while at the same time, making it all clear. There was harmony in all the creatures of the earth - all, that is, except humans. Humans were set apart, different - the dominant species. She laughed to herself at that. Down here, walking the beach, the natural order of species is clear. Humans are dominant yet act like rude guests greedily exploiting their host and overstaying their welcome. She looked down at her watch, and sighed - it was time.

* * * * *

Angela walked into the bus station a few minutes before noon. Crowds of people were rushing about. The hum of activity was resonating all around. Angela saw the lockers against the far wall and walked deliberately towards them. She scanned the crowd nervously. Everyone appeared too busy with their own tasks to notice her. She opened the first empty locker, reached into her pocket, and pulled out the envelope. She took one last look before placing it inside and removing the key.

There were a number of people sitting on benches a few feet away from her and she started towards them. She walked quickly, feeling as though she were pulling a weighted sled. The moment of truth was upon her, and she was a bundle of confused emotions. She felt happy, and sad, and mad, and scared, but it was her nervousness that reigned supreme. "This guy had better be for real", she thought once again.

Finally, she noticed a small, insignificant looking man staring at her. She instinctively looked away, but quickly looked back again. He was holding a bouquet of flowers. He was not at all what she was expecting. The thought crossed her mind that he was probably considered a geek in high school. He wore a T-shirt and jeans that had seen much better days. His hair was long and unkempt and hung down over his heavy black-framed glasses. She noticed the manila envelope on his lap and smiled as she approached. She sat next to him and let out an unconscious sigh.

"Bill?" she asked.

He smiled and put his arm on the backrest behind her, "Angela, I take it?"

"Yes, Bill. Or should I say Dwayne Smythe."

He stopped smiling for a second, and then chuckled. "Should have used a pay phone," he concluded as he shook his head, "No big deal. Did you bring the money?" he asked as he handed her the bouquet of flowers.

She took them instinctively, not really conscious of what she was doing. She nodded her head nervously and looked down at the envelope on his lap, "Is that it?" she asked as she reached for it.

He grabbed the envelope with his free hand. "How stupid do you think I am?"

She didn't answer.

"I saw you at the lockers. You didn't put any money in their, just some envelope," he was definitely angry. "Did you think I wouldn't be watching? What's in the envelope, a letter saying tough luck sucker?"

Angela was decidedly anxious as she looked at Dwayne. She stared him square in the eye, but her voice broke as she spoke, "The bank wouldn't give me that kind of cash. They said it had something to do with regulations. I got you a bank draft made out for the twenty thousand. The payee portion is blank. You can fill in whatever name you want. It's as good as cash. Honestly." She was desperate and tears began welling up in her eyes. Her mind was reeling as she thought, "God, no, don't let him leave."

Dwayne calmed down. The story made sense to him, so he pulled his arm from behind her with his palm up, "The key."

Angela's hand was shaking as she placed the key in his waiting hand. He got up and walked over to the locker and opened it. Seeing the bank's logo on the envelope, he pulled it out and opened it. As Angela had said, a bank draft for the twenty thousand dollars was enclosed. He smiled a very satisfied smile, walked back and tossed the manila envelope into her waiting hands. She grabbed it like a junkie receiving her next fix.

Dwayne spoke smugly, "It has been a pleasure doing business with you, Ms. Michails."

She was sobbing quietly as she looked up a Dwayne. Her face was pale and tears escaped her swollen eyes. His tone changed to sympathetic sincerity, "Best of luck to you, I hope you find him, I really do," and he turned to leave.

Angela called out to him, "Wait!"

A little stunned and surprised he turned back to her, definite confusion showing on his face. She looked down at the envelope, and then back at him, "I have to know. How did you get this information? Where did it come from?" She didn't want to ask, but she had to know whether she could rely on it.

Dwayne looked around quickly and noticed a few people looking at him. The activities of the two had caught their attention. Something was happening, and watching and listening to them was better than just sitting doing nothing. He walked back to Angela and sat down beside her. He put his prize in his jacket pocket, and his arm on the backrest behind her. He leaned into her ear as a lover delivering a precious kiss.

He spoke quite immodestly, "I'm into computers. I was working on the systems at the clinic when you were there. I was in the room right next door to you and I heard the whole conversation - everything. I wanted to help you. There, at the ends of my fingers were all the truths. Let's just say I slipped a little backdoor into their system. Nothing to it really," he chuckled to himself. He was pleased with his skillfulness. "When I got home, after the clinic was closed for the day, I accessed their system from my computer. I now know everything about everyone who has ever used their services." He sat back up and laughed out loud. Angela was stunned. Dwayne continued, tapping his pocket, "And now I know the information I have is going to be worth a lot of money."

He got up again and headed out of the depot, whistling a happy tune and strutting like a peacock.

Angela looked at the envelope on her lap, then back at Dwayne as he was heading out, and then back at the envelope once again, "My God, what have I done? Dear God!" She sat there amongst the crowd for what seemed like hours. She felt they were all looking at her, that the whole world was looking at her and judging her. Tears dripped on the unopened envelope as she thought, "How many lives have I just destroyed with my selfishness? How can I possibly look anyone in the face again?"

She finally glanced at her watch - 1:15 p.m. "Damn! Janet!" she thought. She got up quickly and left the depot.

4

Dwayne walked down the street, glancing frequently over his shoulder, fully expecting to see someone following him. When he felt a safe distance from the bus depot and was sure no one had followed him, he stopped and leaned against a building. He was pleased with himself. It was the easiest twenty thousand dollars he had ever made. He laughed at that, "Hell, that is half a year's wages".

He liked how it felt to acquire that kind of money so easily and imagined all the things he could now do. He reached into his pocket and pulled out the envelope. He had to see it again. He stared at it lovingly and gave it an approving kiss.

He believed that with all the information he now had, he would be seeing a lot more envelopes just like this one. He didn't know how many people would pay as easily as Angela, but he was sure many would. Some would probably pay even more. His eyes lit up at that thought. "Next time it will be fifty thousand. Yeah," he thought, "it's got to be worth fifty thousand. There were five thousand names in that system." He quickly did the arithmetic in his head, and laughed out loud. "Oh, yeah, this is going to be a very good year".

His mind wandered back to his previous job with the government. He had had access to so much information then - sensitive, secret information. However, he had been falsely accused of using the government's computers to download pornography and was fired. He had loved that job and didn't know who had set him up or why. He felt computers, unlike women, were the epitome of purity and logic. They responded to his touch without question or doubt. He had always thought women were irrational and illogical and had never had much luck with them

He suddenly remembered the backdoor he had installed in those systems. He had done that so he could work from home. His intention had been as simple and pure as dedication to the job. No one could have known what he had done.

He smiled to himself, "If people will pay for this information, I wonder how much I could get for the stuff in the government's computers." His eyes grew wider thinking of it. He wondered if he would have the guts to do that. He knew he was considering espionage. "That's serious shit. Firing squad type shit." He wondered momentarily, if they still used firing squads. Then he chuckled to himself, "They'd have to find me first." He was feeling invincible.

He looked back at the bank draft in his hand, trying to decide what he was going to do first. He knew not to get too crazy with the money. He would deposit it in the bank and then do a little shopping. He smiled, having decided he was going out tonight. He was going to treat himself to a fine meal. Then he was going to find himself some female companionship. He had money now. He was sure the lack of money was the reason he had always had such bad luck with women. That was about to change. He was sure he would be irresistible now.

Some of the passing pedestrian traffic looked at him standing there. He had been talking to himself. Most thought him a little off, and it showed on their faces. He started walking again still talking to himself as he headed down the street towards his bank. Sympathetic glances followed his course.

As soon as he got home he would try to get back into those government systems. If he could, he thought his life would change forever. "It would serve them right. They deserve it for firing me like that. They owe me. I'll get even with them." He was very pleased with himself. Tonight would be the beginning, the first evening of the rest of his life. The future looked very promising indeed.

* * * * *

The restaurant was as busy as usual. With its fresh, open feel and good staff, Jack's had everything people were looking for when dining out. It was a very popular spot, specializing in great food, a great atmosphere, a great location right next to the beach, and sporting a large outdoor patio area. Like Angela and her mother, Janet liked coming here. It wasn't stuffy like so many other places around town. Even to Janet, the name "Jack's" seemed a little strange for a place such as this. She was on her second martini when Angela came rushing in. Angela looked out of breath as she approached. Some of the other patrons looked up from their meals as she arrived. Her face was as familiar in this place as the menu itself.

"My God, girlfriend, you look like hell," commented Janet.

Angela looked at her and gave her a sarcastic smile, "I'm happy to see you too," and she sat down.

Janet was still concerned, "I'm serious, Ange. What happened to you? You look like you were banged by your dream man before he dumped you."

A bit crude, Angela thought, but Janet always had a way of over-simplifying most things. They had gone through high school together, and were as close as sisters.

Janet had refused to grow up past those high school years. She was very definitely a twenty year old stuck in post-pubescence which, Angela believed, was why Janet didn't have anyone special in her life. She was a very pretty blond who dressed and carried herself like a princess and was always impeccably groomed. When she walked into a room, all the men would fall in line behind her but, inevitably, she would open her mouth and the crowd would dissipate.

Angela called the waiter over as she looked at Janet's drink. "Far too early for one of those," she paused a second to think, "Ah damn, I'll have one anyway. Make it a double." Angela was halfway between hysteria and tears.

Janet was worried about her friend, "Christ, girl, what's this shit?"

In all the years they had known each other, Janet had never seen Angela drink anything other than wine.

The waiter was back with the drink before Angela had regained enough composure to speak, so she gave him a thoughtful "thank you" smile. Taking a sip of her drink, she gasped, "How can you drink this stuff?", and then took another sip.

Janet just smiled, shrugged her shoulders, and took another sip of her own drink. She knew better than to say anything further. Angela would start the conversation when she was ready.

Grabbing her cigarettes, Janet lit one, and handed it to Angela who promptly took a long draw. Her hands shook. "Janet, you know I don't smoke." She took another drag and extinguished the rest. Janet smiled as she finished her own.

Angela took a deep breath, "I met with a man today." She put the still unopened envelope on the table. "He sold me information about my father."

Janet's face went white. "My God," she exclaimed, brushing the floral center piece aside and reaching for the envelope. Angela slammed her hand down hard on top of the envelope, "There's more."

Angela proceeded to recount the entire meeting with Dwayne. She left nothing out. She still hadn't decided what she was going to do and hoped her girlfriend would have some useful insights for her.

The waiter returned with pad in hand, "Have you decided?"

Both women were startled. They thought for a second and then ordered their usual - Chef's Salad.

"My God, Ange. What are you going to do?" Janet started, "You should call the cops on this guy or something. I mean, he can't do that. He could cause some real shit."

Angela eyes started swelling again. She had been agonizing over the same question herself, "If I call them, I will have to give up my father. If I don't, a lot of people are going to be put through hell. Sure, some are going to be thrilled, but many aren't." She started to cry. "Damn it, Janet, I just wanted to know who he was - is. Now look what I've started."

Janet just shook her head, the two girls sat there looking at each other. They stared, as if they were trying to read each other's minds, combining their thoughts telepathically. They tried desperately to come up with some kind of a solution; a panacea.

Janet broke the silence first, "Ange, it's a tough one. Fulfill your dream, or do what you think is morally right." She paused for a second or two, "I guess what I'm saying is, what do you think is right, and what do you think is wrong?"

Angela saw the point to that. "Life is all about choices and people should have the right to choose. They should be able to decide for themselves what is worth knowing. They should think carefully about what information they want and then be prepared to deal with it. After all, once you know a thing, there is no way then not to know it. I have to trust that people can do that - I have to," she thought.

"You're right as usual." Angela smiled at her friend.

Janet looked confused, "Huh?" Had she said something profound?

"I have to trust people's ability to make their own decisions." Angela took another gulp of her drink. The taste made her shiver uncontrollably, and then she continued, "It's not for me to judge what is right or wrong for other people. I have to do what I feel is right for me, and deal with the consequences, whatever they may be." Angela sat up straight in her chair. She had convinced herself.

Janet looked at her, still not sure what had just happened. "Just like that the world is right again. Christ, Ange, you came in here like death warmed over, and laid this crap on me. Then poof, two minutes later everything is fine." Janet shook her head, agitated. "Don't pull this shit, Ange. Nothing has changed. You may be convinced but I'm not so sure."

Angela ignored her friend and ripped open the envelope. There, staring her in the face was her father's name! It was as bold as life. She didn't feel at all the way she had expected. It was almost anti-climatic. She read the name to herself a half dozen times, slowly. Then she said it aloud, "John Simmons." It didn't roll off her tongue, nor was there any special rush. It was just a name. It still didn't mean a thing, and Angela was visibly disappointed.

Janet shook her head, "Well, what the hell did you expect; God-all-mighty or something?" Janet took another sip of her drink. Angela repeated the name again, softer this time, "John Simmons." She was so sure she would have felt something when she had read it. There should be something. "Shouldn't there be pain, or joy, or recognition, or familiarity, or something - anything?" she thought.

Angela looked at her friend with a distant look in her eyes, "That's my father's name, John Simmons."

Janet looked at her, and shook her head, "You're one screwed up lady, Ange".

Angela closed her eyes and leaned forward on the table. She was suddenly drained. She hadn't eaten all day. That combined with the restless night, the emotional roller coaster of the day, and the few quick gulps of gin had taken everything she had to give. She couldn't take any more. She couldn't think and she needed to think

Janet watched Angela's metamorphosis as she finished her own drink. She realized Angela didn't need to be here, lunch would have to wait for another day. She got up, and caught the attention of their server, "Hey, waiter, cancel that order." He was already on his way with the salads in his hands. He looked annoyed as he changed course. Had it been anyone other than these two he would have said something; instead he muttered under his breath as he returned to the kitchen.

Chuckling, Janet took her friends arm in one hand. Seeing Angela's drink still sitting on the table, she grabbed it with her free hand, "You won't need any more of this", she said, as she drank the glass dry.

"Come on, Ange, I'm taking you home." Janet realized what the scene must look like and she glanced around the restaurant. Most people were looking at the two of them and she suddenly felt sorry for Angela, "Come on, Ange. Work with me. Everyone's staring at you."

Angela didn't respond and stood quietly while Janet settled the bill. The waiter glanced at Angela, clearly concerned. Janet saw it, and looked at Angela, chuckling. "Some girls can't handle martinis in the afternoon." She laughed apologetically and continued escorting Angela out to her own car. Janet shoved Angela in to the back seat unceremoniously then drove away.

* * * * *

Even before Dwayne walked through the door the sounds emanating from inside reached his ears. He liked the sound of the steady drone of noise pounding through the exterior walls. It was like life itself, a powerful heart thundering inside the chest.

He looked himself over as best he could. Everything he had on was new. The soft Italian leather jacket draped over the white silk shirt and blue silk tie. The new dark blue wool pants were punctuated at the waist by an eel skin belt. The ensemble was anchored by black Florsheim shoes on his feet and a gold Esquire on his wrist. He looked the classic three dressed up as a nine.

He was glad he had gone shopping that day. He believed his fine new clothes made him look good and, as a result, he was feeling great. This new found confidence and self-esteem enveloped him as he continued into the club.

He was convinced that tonight was the night. He was sure that here he would be able to find a special someone to help fill that gnawing void in his life – a female companion. The pent up frustrations of years of going it alone had culminated to an almost fever pitch. He could feel the music pounding inside him. It pounded at his very core. His eyes grew wider, his heart started to beat faster and harder. The hidden animal that lurked in his human spirit started to rise to the surface. He began to feel the hunger of the hunter.

Scanning the room, he observed the antics of the crowd. The dance floor was packed with gyrating bodies responding to the rhythm of the numbing beat. Others huddled around tables, smiling. Some were watching the activities on the dance floor intently, while others were engaged in seemingly futile têtê à têtê.

The scene brought a smile to his face as he thought, "The man beast still lives and this place is the purist example of it."

From his position across the room, his scan picked up a young woman standing beside the bar. Suddenly, everyone else in the club seemed to simply fade to translucent periphery. All his senses focused on her, certain she was the most beautiful creature he had ever seen.

She was a red headed beauty sporting an exquisite salon tan. Her hazel eyes seemed to pierce right through him even though her gaze was directed at the dance floor and not at him at all. She hadn't noticed him, but he knew she soon would.

As he approached her, he visualized her standing on some seashore, the bright sun reflecting off her eyes, and her long dress fluttering in the breeze. She looked like an angel sent to earth just for him. He felt grateful and wanted to thank someone for her.

His approach seemed to take forever. What would he say once he reached her? He didn't know, but hoped he wouldn't make too big a fool of himself. Finally beside her, his most sincere smile fixed, he cleared his throat. "Would you like to dance?" He replayed that sentence over in his mind seemingly a hundred times, unsure if that had been the right approach, but it was done.

She pulled her eyes off the dance floor and looked toward the voice. She smiled when she saw the beads of sweat on his forehead, and then glanced back at the dance floor shrugging her shoulders, "Sure, why not?"

The sound of her voice made his heart skip a beat. It was the sweetest melody on earth. He was now certain he was in love.

She put her drink on the bar and took his waiting arm as they proceeded to the dance floor. He knew his dancing was bad. He had not had many opportunities to perfect his technique. Now he just wanted to get off the floor and go where they could just sit and talk. But, equal to his desire to retreat, was his desire to stay. He was enjoying watching her move. She was a much better dancer than he and, in his opinion, better than anyone else in the room. Her motions made his heart feel larger, and the feeling in his stomach was a hunger, a fear, yet warm. He wanted her more than anything.

The song ended far too quickly, and she mouthed a "Thank you" at him and walked, unescorted, back to the bar and her drink. He felt sadness as she walked away. "That can't be it," he muttered under his breath and followed her.

Once back at the bar she ordered a new drink. He pulled a three dollar cigarillo from his shirt pocket, and lit it from a book of matches displaying the club's logo. When he had purchased it, he had thought the cigarillo would make him look sophisticated. However, he wasn't a smoker and as he inhaled deeply he began to choke.

The sounds of his choking made her turn. She smiled and chuckled openly as she saw him fighting his own body's rejection of the smoke. He was embarrassed as he reached past her and put the thing out in an ashtray on the bar.

Once it was thoroughly extinguished, he looked back at her and smiled. "I'm kind of new at all this." He let out a sheepish chuckle. "Listen, this place is a little noisy. Would you like to go somewhere a little quieter and have a coffee or something?"

He was sure she must be entranced by him. There was absolutely no reason for her not to go with him. She would, of course, have been waiting for the offer. In his mind, she was desperately hoping he would ask her.

She looked him up and down, sizing him up; trying to see what was really there in front of her. His face was still that of a little boy, yet his clothes suggested wealth. She wanted to tell him to go away, but accepted the invitation instead. With a feigned smile, she spoke, "Yeah sure, why not? Any place in mind?"

She wasn't sure if it was pity or charity that had made her accept. She knew it wasn't attraction. Maybe, it was simply her own loneliness that was clouding her judgment, maybe a form of desperation that lurked inside her made her accept the first invitation she got.

He smiled knowingly. He had been sure she would accept. How could she not be totally overwhelmed by his charms? "How about my place?" His grin was wide and somewhat ominous.

She saw it and didn't care. She put her drink back on the bar thinking it wasn't too late to change her mind as she turned to his waiting arm. She spoke in a matter-of-fact tone, "My name is Lisa."

He thought how incredibly beautiful her name was. He said her name over and over in his mind, "Lisa. Lisa. Lisa. Lisa Smythe." He liked the sound of it. It made him feel very good indeed. "I'm Dwayne. Dwayne Smythe."

She shook her head internally, "Dwayne. That figures." The name disgusted her but she wasn't sure why. She had known Dwaynes in the past and every one had been very nice. Hearing that name coming from his mouth just sounded repulsive but she followed his lead out of the club.

* * * * *

As the two approached the front of his building, she hesitated, looking at the façade. It certainly wasn't what she had been expecting. It was rather plain, not the elaborate address she had imagined. She considered leaving again, but continued forward.

On reaching his apartment, she looked around. It was nice enough and clearly a male's apartment - purely functionally and without character - yet it was clean and neat. She decided it was as positive a sign of good character as anything else.

Dwayne saw her inspecting the room and smiled to himself. He was glad he had taken the time to straighten up. It had been some time since he had made that effort. He had known that tonight he would have company and had felt an urge to make the place a little more presentable. His decision had been right. He broke the silence first, "Lisa, make yourself comfortable. I'll get us some wine."

She interrupted her scan and looked towards him and smiled, "That would be nice. Where's your powder room, I'd like to freshen up."

They were the first words she had spoken since they left the club. In the silence of his apartment, they resounded like the finest bells in the grandest church. He believed he could sit and listen to her talk for an eternity. He pointed toward the small hallway that led to the back of the apartment, "First door on the left," and he continued to the kitchen. She smiled at his back and headed for the privacy of that room.

Standing there, looking at herself in the mirror, she began to shake her head. She wasn't pleased with the image she saw. "What the hell are you doing here?" The reflection didn't answer her. It didn't have to, she knew, and closed her eyes momentarily sighing. "What the hell? He's a creep, but he's alive and warm. He'll do."

In the privacy of that room she began to disrobe. Every piece of clothing came off except her shoes. She stood now completely naked and looked at herself in the mirror. She smiled at the image before her. Her body was beautiful and she enjoyed gazing upon herself.

She had always gone to great lengths to watch her diet, and engaged in a regular regime of exercise. It all showed in that mirror. Every inch of her was firm and in perfect proportion. The tanning sessions had paid off, not a tan line anywhere. She looked at herself from every possible angle and smiled. She was a real living work of art. The great sculptors would have been truly inspired had they had her for their subject.

A man's voice reached her ear, "Are you okay in there?" She suddenly remembered where she was and who belonged to the voice. She sighed, and shook her head. "What a waste." She took one more, quick look at herself, and spoke loud enough for him to hear, "Yeah, I'm coming."

She gathered up her things neatly and opened the door. Taking a deep breath, she walked back into the living room. Dwayne was standing in the middle of room holding two glasses of red wine. On seeing her, his jaw dropped, his eyes grew large, and the glasses shattered on the floor.

The effect she had had on him made her smile proudly as she tossed her garments on a chair. She looked back at him still standing in shock. She spoke as softly and seductively as she could "Listen, Dwayne, we both know why we're here. So what say we just cut the formalities and get to it?"

He was only marginally able to compose himself and a broad smile grew across his face. He pointed down the hall towards his bedroom. She smiled back at him and headed in the direction he had indicated. He was close behind.

His bedroom was essentially the same as the rest of the apartment, neat and sparse. However, the bank of computers along one wall captured her attention. She had a PC at home like most people, but here, he had five different units. She was genuinely surprised to see them. She turned back to him, "Why so many?"

He thought to himself momentarily. In his mind, she was going to be a life-long companion, so he decided there was no reason not to tell her of his plans. A sinister smile came over his face as he outlined his activities and the information to which he now had access. He was so absorbed in his story he completely forgot that the woman in front of him was completely naked.

Lisa listened intently. His passion for the plan was in his voice. Her eyes grew wider as she began to realize the money he would be making, the power he possessed, the possibility of her sharing in it all - she was aroused. The fire inside her began to grow. The thought of it was endearing this man to her, and she now wanted him totally. She reached out as he continued to speak and dragged him to the bed. They made love all night long. Not the loving, passionate coupling enjoyed by caring people, but rather an angry, savage, ravenous, animal sex. The barrier between pleasure and pain was ignored.

5

Angela's eyes opened. As her focus returned, she glanced at her watch - 10:07 p.m. She moaned as she shook her head. Then she remembered her friend bringing her home. "Have a nap, girlfriend. I'll see you tomorrow," Janet had said when she left.

Angela remembered sitting alone on the couch and finishing half a bottle of wine. So much had been going through her mind and the wine calmed the chaos of her thoughts. Now, as she was waking, her head was paying the price of the liquid tranquilizer.

Elaine saw her daughter stirring as she came down the stairs and entered the living room. "Ah, you're awake. Good. Janet called me at work and told me what happened. You couldn't leave well enough alone, could you?" Her mother was almost angry, almost sympathetic.

Angela thought, "Let me wake up first," as she sat up and wiped the sleep from her eyes. "How long have I been out?"

"You were exhausted", Elaine pointed to a tray of cheese and crackers on the coffee table, "Have something to eat, dear. You must be famished"

Angela shook her head, and brushed the hair out of her face, "Let's just get on with it." She knew her mother had a few things to say. She had noticed the papers sitting on the coffee table next to the cheese tray and believed her mother must have read them.

"John Simmons," Elaine started, "So that's his name," and calmly reached for the papers. Angela thought, "Too calm!"

Elaine continued, "He must be 43 by now. Seven years younger than me. For some reason I thought he would be older." She chuckled quietly at that. "From this," still looking at the papers, "it appears he lives just on the other side of town. That is if he still lives there." She looked at her daughter, "It was more than twenty years ago. I'm sure he has moved by now. What is it they say? The average person moves every five years. Something like that." She looked at her daughter, "So what is your plan now, dear. Are you going to drop by his home for a visit" Her voice was noticeably sarcastic.

"Don't be mad, Mom." Angela's eyes were starting to tear up again. "You know how important this is to me."

"Yes, dear, I do know." Elaine softened, "I wish you had told me about that Dwayne fellow. He was the one that called last night, wasn't he?"

Angela looked at the floor, "Yes," then suddenly she looked back at her mother, and stiffened up, "It was him. It cost me twenty thousand dollars, and you know what? I really don't care. I really don't."

She had just come to the realization that she really didn't care. She didn't care about anything else right now. She was more convinced and determined than ever. She had to know. She wasn't going to let anything stop her from pursuing this; nothing - and no one.

Elaine saw her determination and resolve. Putting her arm around her, she drew her daughter's head to her own chest as if it were a child's, "My dear sweet Angela."

Tears shone in Elaine's eyes. "I have wondered about him myself over the years. I've wondered who he was. Not like you, of course, but curious. You're my beautiful baby. Who was the man that helped me create such a beautiful creature?" She paused and tried to push her emotions away. It was the first time she had ever said those words out loud and now, she wasn't sure she should have. She felt perhaps she was showing weakness and it bothered her. Her strong side surfaced again, "You will tell me about him?"

Elaine could feel her daughter's head nod against her chest. The two sat there, silently holding each other. They both knew that tomorrow could change their lives forever. It was inevitable. They were both happy and terrified.

* * * * *

It had been an anxious day for Philip. He enjoyed these trips, but the long meetings always tensed him up. He felt the need to relax and unwind, and stopping at the hotel's bar for a couple drinks at the end of the day was not an unusual event. Nor was it unusual for him to be joined by someone to help him ease his tensions. Even on this trip, knowing his wedding was only days away, he felt the desire for some female companionship. In his mind he did love Angela, but this was different. This wasn't about love, it was recreation. His success had delivered him to this position in life, and he believed he deserved rewards. "Besides," he thought, "no one will ever know."

Now a few hours later, Philip collapsed, satisfied and depleted. "She's a beautiful woman," he thought, as he looked into her face. She was barely twenty-two, a decade his junior. He could feel her wonderful proportioned body wet and firm against his and he smiled.

She was like so many women he had known before - pretty and willing. Right now, he wasn't sure he could remember her name. He was a modern hunter but his trophies wouldn't be hung on a wall, but rather linger in a special vault within his mind - his memories. They lay there for several minutes in the dark, recovering and listening to the sound of the rain falling outside.

She broke the calm first, "When can we get together again?" She spoke so softly that he had almost missed it.

He thought, "Oh, oh, here it comes."

This was always the hardest part, "Actually, I rarely make it here. This is the first time I have been here in many years." For a moment, Philip couldn't remember what town he was in. He looked into her face again, "Make sure I get your number. You never know, I may be back soon." He was attempting sincerity but it didn't work.

She looked into his eyes carefully. She saw what she had expected to see and what she had hoped she wouldn't see. It was the same old thing she had seen far too many times - nothing at all. She rolled away from him and got out of bed. As she headed for the bathroom, she looked back at him, "Yeah sure, Philip. I'll do that. I'll leave it on the nightstand for you."

She didn't mean it. She had hoped maybe, just maybe, this time would be different. When she returned to the room, she started to dress. He watched as she put on her things. "Poetry in motion," he thought. He truly loved women and the way they moved - even when they were as angry as this one.

As she finished dressing, she looked at the mirror and tried to fix her hair. It wasn't working. Frustrated she gave up and headed for the door. As she opened it, she looked back to the bed one more time. He was propped up on one elbow and smiling at her. She faked a smile back. "See you around Philip," and the door closed behind her. Philip rolled onto his back and he stared at the ceiling. He didn't feel happy, or sad, only satisfied as he drifted off to sleep.

Lisa pulled off the blonde wig she was wearing releasing her dyed red hair from its confines as she headed back down to the hotel's bar. She had been a little tipsy when she had gone to his room, but now the buzz and numbness were fading. She was starting to feel again and didn't much care for that. She took the same stool as she had occupied earlier and ordered another drink.

She had spent far too many nights this way and there had been far too many broken promises. Too many men treating her the way Philip just had was taking its toll on her. Lisa didn't like the way she was feeling and she was sure Philip was the reason.

She had planned this whole meeting. Knowing he would be here, she planted herself for him to discover. What bothered her most was that Philip didn't have a clue who she was. She could have told him many times, but didn't. She wanted desperately to be with him and had succeeded in that at least. In the time they had spent together, she had hoped that he would recognize her and everything would be fine. It simply didn't happen.

It was then she remembered the camera and she smiled. A few more drinks would take away the depression; a few more and she would be able to think clearly.

* * * * *

Angela awoke and stared at the ceiling. Stretching, she rolled over and looked at the clock; 8:15 a.m. She thought and smiled, "I'm glad I took this time off," and closed her eyes again. The plans of the day rushed through her mind. She sighed as she got out of bed and headed for the shower. The warm water felt good against her skin. She stood motionless for some time and let the hard stream caress her. She likened the feeling to the hands of a skillful masseuse bringing life to her wakening body.

Choosing what to wear was going to be a challenge. She had to look just right. She reviewed her entire wardrobe in her mind as she applied her make-up. Looking at herself in the mirror, she chuckled, "What was it Philip had said? Women spend so much time and money on their make-up, all so they can look natural" Her smile left. "Philip," she thought, "He's coming back at 2:00 p.m. today. Damn." She'd deal with that later.

When she was satisfied with her appearance, she headed downstairs to the living room. It was time. As she picked up the papers from the coffee table, she thought, "Mom's probably right. It's been twenty years. He's probably moved," and reached for the phone book instead.

Sitting on the couch with the book on her lap, Angela took a deep breath and opened it to the "S's". "Simmons. Simmons," she said, under her breath, "Ah, here we go, Simmons A, Simmons Brad, Simmons Henry," her finger ran down the page, her heart pounding, "Simmons Henry, Simmons Ken, Simmons Stanley." She paused, and then looked it over again. "No John." She looked again, "I don't believe it. No J... No John. He's not here."

She sat back in the couch, "Now what?" She had been so sure this was going to be easy. In her mind, he was sitting beside the phone waiting for her to call. How naïve! For the first time she realized he wasn't expecting to hear from her - ever. In fact, he didn't even know she existed and was living a life that had nothing to do with her.

Her mother had been right. Not only had he moved, but he had actually left town. She became more determined now than ever, the thought of quitting never entered her mind. It seemed like he was daring her to find him. She was certain she would find him, but she couldn't think how.

"Janet," she thought and reached for the phone.

"Hello," Janet sounded half asleep.

"Hi, Janet. Ange. Did I wake you?" She glanced at the clock on the mantle. 10:00 a.m.

"Not at all, Ange. I had to get up and answer the phone anyway." There was definite sarcasm in Janet's voice, "What's up? How are you feeling today?"

Angela paused for a few seconds to let Janet wake up a little more. "Ange? Are you there?" Janet sounded annoyed.

"Yes, sweetie, I'm here. Just waiting for you to join the world." she chuckled to herself. Janet was not a morning person, but Angela always felt better hearing her voice, and continued, "I'm feeling much better. I'm doing great."

Angela paused briefly, gathering her thoughts, "Listen, Janet. I've got a bit of a problem." Janet immediately chuckled, and Angela ignored it. "I've been looking through the book. There's no listing for John Simmons. Do you have any suggestions?" Her voice sounded a little shaky and desperate.

Janet replied sarcastically, "Oh, yeah. I've got a few suggestions for you!"

Angela pushed, "Janet!"

Janet softened her tone, "Sorry, girlfriend. Let me think." Janet paused, giving the question consideration,

"Where do you go when you want to find someone, and it's been twenty years," thinking aloud.

Angela perked up. She was almost screaming into the phone, "Janet, you're a genius! I knew I should call you! I'll talk to you later! Thanks! Love you! Bye!" and she hung up the phone.

Janet was somewhat stunned as she stared at the phone in her hand. She muttered under her breath, "Jesus Christ, Ange! Sure glad I woke up for that!" She slammed the receiver into its cradle and headed back to bed, "Bloody middle of the night!"

Angela opened the yellow pages to the "D's". A quarter page professional looking ad caught her attention:

Johnson and Johnson Detective Agency
Engagements, divorces, surveillance, and missing persons.

"That says it all," she thought, as she tapped the number into the phone.

A female voice answered, "Good morning. Johnson and Johnson Detective Agency, Carol speaking. How may I direct your call?" Carol sounded very professional.

"Hi, my name is Angela Michails. I'd like to talk to someone about a missing person." Her voice was equally calm and professional.

"Certainly, Ms. Michails," Carol paused for a second, as she looked over the appointment book. It was empty. "How does two o'clock today sound?" Carol tried to make it appear as if they were a busy firm.

Angela had been convinced by the charade as she thought of Philip's arrival time, "Yes. 2:00 p.m. sounds fine."

"Very good, Ms. Michails, we'll see you then," and the phone went dead.

Angela hung up and thought for a couple of seconds, then dialed again.

"Hello."

"Hi, Mike. Ange."

"Well, hello there sweetheart," Mike was pleased to hear Angela's voice. He was Philip's best friend and was to be the best man at the wedding. Mike and Philip have known each other since school and Mike was the only person Philip had ever trusted. Mike generally referred to himself as an entrepreneur, which in his case meant he couldn't hold a job. He made his living any way he could and that usually involved something sleazy.

"You're finally calling to tell me you dumped that loser and you're ready to move up?" There was a jovial tone to Mike's voice. Angela had never liked him, but knew he was kidding. She had always thought that Mike considered himself God's gift to the world.

"Listen, Mike," she was using her sweetest voice, "Something really important has come up. I have to take a meeting this afternoon. Can you do me a favor and pick up Philip at the airport?"

"Sure, sweet cheeks. I'd be glad to. The old boy off globe trotting again, was he?"

"Thanks Mike. You're a dear. His flight arrives at two. I really appreciate this. Tell Philip I love him and I'll give him a call after dinner."

Mike chuckled, "Anything for you, doll. Maybe I can take it out in trade?" Mike was only half kidding.

Angela took a condescending tone, "Bye, Mike." She hung up the phone thinking, "What a pig." She looked down at her watch, "Damn, where is this day going?" She was supposed to be at the lawyer's office at 11:00 a.m., and now she would have to hurry.

The receptionist looked up and smiled as Angela burst through the door, "Good day, Ms. Michails."

A nicely dressed gentleman was sitting in the reception area leafing through a magazine. He looked up, startled by her entrance. Seeing Angela's frantic state, he chuckled knowingly and went back to his magazine.

"Hi Sandy, sorry I'm late. Is he mad?" Angela was noticeably out of breath.

Sandy had already picked up the phone and buzzed in. She said something inaudible into the receiver and then hung it up. Looking back at Angela, she smiled, "He's been expecting you. Go right in."

Angela had been in these offices many times in the past and had always been impressed by them. They were modern in design, and very tastefully decorated. The best description would be "Modern conservatism". The office was very professional in appearance, but one didn't feel a lot of pockets had been emptied to pay for it.

Angela, generally, didn't care for lawyers, but Simon had been a family friend for many years. He had handled their affairs since her parents had been married. He had been there during her father's funeral and for weeks afterward. He looked after the business until Elaine was able to get back to work, and he had never been paid for any of it, saying it was the least he could do. Angela had never really understood what that meant and her mother had never said.

In fact, Angela hadn't known, until recently, how great his sacrifice had been. He had lost his own practice because of it and had come to work for this firm a year later. He was now a senior partner and although he had never mentioned it, she felt he had no regrets.

When Angela entered his office, Simon was standing in front of his glass topped desk. He had a very pleasant smile on his face and his right hand was out stretched in greeting. Angela had always liked him.

He was in his late 50's. His head supported thick salt and pepper hair, and his six foot frame was that of a linebacker. His presence seemed to fill the room. She had often thought her father would have looked like him. She took his hand and continued forward and gave him a hug and a peck on his neck, "Always good to see you, Mr. Bonder."

"I'm glad to see too, Angela", and he gave her a gentle kiss on the top of her head. "How many times have I told you to call me Simon?" His voice was pleasant to her ears.

She backed away from him, and sat in one of the wing chairs that faced his desk. In all the years she had known him, she couldn't bring herself to be that informal with him. She wasn't sure why. Respect or something, she had guessed. It would be like calling her mother by her first name and she couldn't do that either. Simon moved to the opposite side of the desk and pulled himself up close to it.

"Tell me," he started, his voice deep and sweet, "How's your mother doing?"

Angela smiled, "She's great. Busy as usual. You know."

He smiled and nodded. Simon had never married and was very fond of Elaine. He had taken her out socially on a number of occasions over the years. He had hoped to develop a serious relationship with her, but knew it was unlikely. Still, he never gave up hope.

Angela had been aware of Simon's feelings for her mother and had talked to Elaine about him on several occasions. Angela believed they would have made a good couple, but her mother always had an excuse for not getting involved.

He continued, "And that spinney friend of yours - Janet is it?"

Angela chuckled, "Oh, Janet's Janet."

He was being more cordial than actually caring when he had asked about her. She was a good friend to Angela and that was the only reason he ever inquired about her. "The wedding plans are going well?" The timbre of his voice was far more serious this time.

Angela smiled proudly, "Yes, Great. I think I'm ready. There are only a few more days to go." Angela had been planning her wedding since she was a little girl. She had the whole affair pictured in her mind. She envisioned how beautifully the church would be decorated and how everyone would be dressed. She had imagined all the sounds, all the sights, and all the smells. Now that the day was actually approaching, she was confident that everything was going to be exactly as she had imagined.

Simon opened the file on his desk as he looked at Angela, "You're sure this prenuptial agreement is all right with you?"

She smiled back at him, "It's not a very romantic thing to be doing, granted, but I can understand Philip's lawyers." There was no doubt in her mind that this was their idea and not his.

Simon leaned back in his chair and crossed his arms in front of him, "So can I, of course. If I were Philips' lawyer, I would recommend the same thing. The man has amassed millions and he should protect them. Marriages are like business partnerships in many ways. They always start out happy and carefree, but sometimes things happen. It's sad, but it is reality." He looked at her.

He realized that the analogy wasn't particularly appropriate. "I'm sorry, Angela. I personally don't like these things. I agree with their importance, and I have recommended them on many occasions myself, but I still don't like them."

Angela nodded in agreement. "This thing does protect both of us?"

"Yes, Angela," Simon nodded confidently, "I went over it personally and very thoroughly. You are offered the same protection as he is. His estate is protected and so is yours. And, of course, in the event that one of you dies, the survivor inherits the other's entire estate. There are no surprises in it, just the standard language." He paused for a second, "Well as standard as these things can be."

Angela trusted him implicitly. Simon had said he went over it personally and that was good enough for her. She had assumed an associate would normally have done that kind of thing, but she believed Mr. Bonder took everything that affected her and her mother personally. She reached for a pen and the file.

Simon used a cautious tone, "Aren't you at least going to look it over." He was genuinely surprised by her eagerness.

Angela smiled confidently as she looked into his eyes. She shook her head, and flipped to the last page of each copy. It was done.

Simon smiled politely at her and closed the file. Angela sat back in her chair, feeling nothing at all.

6

Philip was standing at the baggage carousel when Mike walked up to him. "Hey, Phil. Good trip?"

Philip turned to face him, "Hey, Mickey. It was okay. You know how much I dislike these trips. I hate kissing the ass of some self-righteous asshole for days at a time. Wining and dining some jerk I'd rather take out behind the shed. Sometimes I wonder why I hired a sales staff at all." Philip grabbed his bag off the carousel. A man in a business suit was standing next to him watching for his own bag. He looked up at Philip disapprovingly. Philip looked back at him and sneered.

Mike chuckled, "So why'd you go then?"

Philip smiled, "He's one of my biggest and oldest customers. Every now and then I have to go down and stroke him personally to keep him happy." They both laughed. The other man smiled and shook his head as he walked towards the exit. Clearly he had just been on a similar trip.

Mike and Philip had been friends since their school days. Philip was constantly getting into fights in the school yard. Even then, Mike had a powerful build and very quick hands and he had always come to Philip's defense. As a result, Philip tried to take care of Mike in his own way. He couldn't remember how much money he had loaned Mike over the years, and he didn't care. They had always needed each other, a virtual Yin and Yang - like brothers, only closer.

Philip knew that Mike wouldn't be able to handle working for him and therefore never offered him a job. However, whenever Mike had a scheme or idea for making money, Philip would provide the revenue to initiate it. He had never believed in any of Mike's ideas, but felt he had to support them. Now in his thirties, Mike's body was starting to soften and spread. His hands were a little slower, his disposition a little angrier, yet Philip loved him and he knew he would always be there for him. Philip sincerely believed that without his help, Mike wouldn't survive.

Mike continued, slapping his friend on the shoulder, "Any new trophies you want to tell me about."

Philip smiled and looked around to make sure no one else was listening, "You know I don't kiss and tell."

Mike smiled back, "Yeah, right! Who was she? Anyone I might be interested in?"

Philip laughed from his belly, "No." and shook his head, "She was way out of your league. She still had a pulse!"

Mike laughed back as he pointed to the Arrivals exit and they followed the stream of people out the door.

"Where's Angela?" Philip asked.

Mike shook his head and let out a half laugh, "Dammit Evans. You can talk about your accomplishments and ask about your fiancée, all in one sentence." Mike shook his head again and chuckled, "You're a man after my own heart!" He paused for a second and put his hand on Philip's shoulder, "She's at home resting. I worked her pretty hard while you were away. She's worn out." Mike laughed harder this time.

Philip was visibly annoyed. He didn't like anyone making jokes about Angela - especially Mike. Philip was very much in love with Angela. He always made a distinction in his mind between love and sex. He truly believed one meant everything, the other meant nothing. He was concerned now for mentioning it to Mike, "You won't say anything to Angela? If she found out, she'd kill me."

Mike laughed, "You don't think she'd let you off that easy, do you?"

They both laughed, "No, I don't suppose she would."

"Besides, I'd never tell anyone our little secrets, you know that." Philip was again confident Mike would stay quiet. Mike had never told anyone before and Philip had no reason to think this time would be any different.

Mike knew he had crossed the line with his comments about Angela and took a more serious tone, "Sorry man, about what I said. Angela asked me to tell you that something important had come up. She had to take a meeting or something. She'd call you tonight. Okay?"

Philip smiled at him, "Thank you." He wasn't just thanking him for relaying the message, but also for the apology. Philip hoped Angela's absence wasn't for anything too serious. He knew how dedicated a person she was; to her there were no trivial things. That was one of her characteristics he loved.

Outside the white limousine was waiting. Seeing it, Philip looked at Mike, "Shit man. Why'd you bring that thing? You know how much I hate it. I only bought it to impress the clients."

Mike laughed and slapped Philip's shoulder, "Yeah, I know. I'm impressed, too. I love it. I look good riding in it. Besides, I like your champagne. It's free." He laughed again. Philip just shook his head and got in. Mike followed him, grabbing his half empty glass from the small tray.

A small crowd had gathered around the car. Pretending not to care, each was trying to see who it was getting into the car. Maybe it was someone famous - a celebrity. They wore their disappointment on their faces.

The driver placed Philip's bag in the trunk and they drove off.

* * * * *

Angela stood in front of the aged building looking at the piece of paper in her hand. "It's the right place all right." she thought.

Remembering the sound of Carol's voice and the way she had handled herself, Angela was surprised at the appearance of this façade. She expected the inside of the building to look better, but it didn't. She walked up the dimly lit staircase and down the hallway. The route was lit only by bare bulbs hanging from the ceiling. She couldn't imagine a time when this building had ever looked nice. She came to a door marked, Johnson and Johnson Detective Agency. She shook her head and entered.

The room was clean enough, but it was obvious that the wood paneling and floors were original. There were a couple of chairs against one wall, and a couple filing cabinets against another. The lovely old light fixture that hung from the ceiling caught Angela's attention; it was the only thing in the room that appealed to her. Behind the oak desk in front of her sat a pretty woman in her mid-thirties. Although a little over made-up, she was attractive.

"Carol is it?" Angela started politely.

Carol had a nice smile, "That's right. You must be Ms. Michails? Have a seat. Dick will be right with you."

Angela giggled as she retreated to one of the chairs, "Dick Johnson", she thought. "It couldn't be."

It was only a matter of seconds before the door behind Carol opened and a man appeared. He was easily in his mid-forties. He looked rough, figuratively and literally speaking; a man that had seen too much and done too much. He was wearing a brown tweed sport jacket with a black T-shirt and black slacks. He looked presentable, but she couldn't help wondering if his socks matched.

"Ms. Michails, please come in," he smiled warmly. His voice was strong and confident, yet his smile looked out of place.

Angela followed him into his office. Dick took a cloth and brushed off the chair in front of his desk. Angela looked quite stunning in her outfit, and he felt an obligation to clean up for her. Angela didn't believe the chair was dirty, but she was touched by his gesture anyway. She sat down without giving it another thought. Dick moved to his own side of the desk, "So, Ms. Michails, what brings you to my part of the sewer?"

"I saw your ad in the Yellow Pages. Your rec... Carol sounded so professional on the phone and Johnson and Johnson sounded like a professional organization." She looked around his office again. Her impression from the phone certainly didn't suggest a place like this. She knew that had not been the answer to the question he asked but she was interested to hear his response.

He was still standing, and thrust his hips forward, "Me and my partner go everywhere together," and he laughed.

Angela was immediately disgusted and spoke sharply, "That's it" and got up to leave.

Dick put his hand up in front of himself, "Wait. I'm sorry. That wasn't very funny. With a handle like Dick Johnson, I had to develop a particular sense of humor - I have to be able to laugh. You can understand that I'm sure. I apologize. Please, sit, let's start over." Angela nodded politely, not really sure she wanted to continue.

Dick spoke sarcastically, "I don't know what my parents were thinking. My name is Richard." He shook his head, "They must have known."

He paused for a second realizing he had swayed off topic again. "I don't apologize for my ad, or the way Carol handles herself. Look around. We don't get much walk in traffic. That stuff works. When people get to the point that they need someone like me, they look in the phone book and see my ad. They call and get Carol. By the time she's done, they're sold. They have already decided to hire me before they ever get here. Am I wrong? You're still here."

Angela thought, "Not for much longer if this doesn't start going somewhere." She was starting to relax though and could sense something special about him.

Dick saw her apprehension as he sat down and cupped his fingers together on his desk. "Ms. Michails. May I call you Angela?" He waited for her nod before continuing, "Angela, I assure you I am a professional. I have been doing this for a very long time and I am very good at what I do."

Angela believed him.

He continued, "I was a cop - a detective - for 15 years. There isn't much in this world I haven't seen. This life is all I know."

Angela wasn't surprised to hear that. He sat quietly, obviously reflecting on his past. Then he sat further back in his chair and looked Angela in the eye, "Let's face it, you're not the kind of person I generally get in here." She chuckled as she tried to imagine who a typical client might be.

"Five years ago," he continued, staring into space, "my partner and I were on a case. The specifics aren't important. We were checking out an apartment and I didn't notice a man pointing a gun at me from a dark corner. He had me dead in his sights." He paused shaking his head.

"My partner saw him, jumped, and knocked me out of the way just as the gun went off." Relaying this story was obviously hard for him.

"The bullet took half of Frank's head clean off. That stupid bastard. He died right there on top of me. He saved my miserable life."

He paused again then shook his head, "I lost it. I flipped out. I attacked that bastard. I took a bullet in the leg on the way to him and I didn't even feel it. I literally beat that son of a bitch to death with my bare hands. I was so..." He looked back into Angela's eyes. Angela could see his pain and believed that pain and guilt held him together and got him through his days.

He refocused before continuing, "They said it was self defense. It was probably a good thing I had been hit or else... Anyway, I hit the bottle pretty hard. I was drunk for two years. I stopped going to work, my wife left. I just threw it all away."

The images were strong in her mind and she was feeling a little sorry for him. None of this was her business and she hoped he would stop.

He continued, "Eventually I got myself back together. I was able to climb out of the gutter to this charming place." He laughed out loud.

He wasn't really sure why he had told her his story. He rarely talked about it. Something about her made him feel the need to justify himself. Besides, business had been pretty slow since, well, forever. He wasn't really prepared to let this client get away without a fight.

Angela sat silently staring at him. She had decided to stay, she wasn't sure if it was confidence in him or pity. She tossed the file on the desk, and told him her story. As she told it, she felt how insignificant it was in comparison to what he had been through. However, she did feel he would understand and was confident he would be able to help her.

Angela concluded, "So you see. I would really like you to find him before next weekend."

Dick laughed at that, "No problem! Shiiiit!" He paused, shaking his head, "It could take me a couple of hours to find this guy. It could take months. Hell, it could take years. You really haven't given me much to work with here. I'm good, but you have to be realistic."

Angela got up confidently, "Then, Richard," she now felt compelled to call him Richard. "I suggest you get started," and she turned and left.

Richard smiled, he always enjoyed looking at women as they walked away, but there was something different about Angela. His usual leers were absent as he thought of how nice his name sounded when she said it.

* * * * *

Elaine answered the phone. "Well hello Philip." There was a pause. "Yes, she's right here," and she held the phone out in front of her.

Angela walked quickly over and took the receiver to her ear, "Hi, sweetheart. How was your trip?" She was almost cooing.

She laughed at his response. She knew how much he enjoyed those trips, even if he wouldn't admit it.

"No. Not tonight. I'm exhausted. I think I'm just going to have a glass of wine and go to bed."

She laughed again, "You're bad."

A more serious tone came over her, "Oh, yeah. Everything's fine. I'll tell you all about it tomorrow, Okay?"

She was relieved at not having to relive the whole day again, "Thanks, sweetheart. Talk to you tomorrow. I love you." She hung up the phone and returned to her chair in front of the fire. She had noticed something in his voice. She wasn't sure what it was but she had heard it before.

* * * * *

Angela and Janet were deep in conversation when Lisa arrived wearing a pleasant smile on her tanned face. Her skin color amplified her red hair. She was a strikingly beautiful woman.

Angela had a special place in her heart for Lisa. Angela cared for all her friends, but Lisa had been through so much hurt over the years. Angela often thought of the things that had happened in Lisa's life. It was those thoughts that often fueled Angela's thankfulness for the life that she had been fortunate enough to live.

Angela smiled as Lisa sat at the table, "Hi, Lisa. What happened to Sheryl?"

This was more than just a girl's lunch. Angela had wanted to discuss the specifics of what she expected of her bridesmaids throughout the wedding. Angela considered this as important a meeting as any she had ever had and was disappointed that Sheryl wasn't there.

Lisa looked at Angela and shook her head. "Her boss has her working through lunch again."

Angela shook her head knowingly, thinking yet again that Sheryl should find another job. Her boss worked her far too hard, but for some reason Sheryl really enjoyed the job and had never thought her boss unreasonable. Maybe her friend had a crush on him or something; why else would she be so dedicated to a louse like him?

Angela spoke cynically, "Well, I hope he gives her the time off for my wedding. It would sure be nice if all my bridesmaids were there. You two aren't going to back out on me, are you?" She chuckled out loud, only half joking. Both of her companions shook their heads acknowledging their commitment to the wedding.

Lisa reached her hand out and touched the top of Angela's, "I wouldn't miss it for the world, sweetheart." and she smiled sweetly.

Angela saw her face, and feeling the touch of her hand, was relieved. It had been almost a year since their big fight. Lisa had been so angry with Angela then. Lisa had had a long time crush on Philip and was devastated when Angela started seeing him. Angela had been certain that it would spell the end of their friendship, but it hadn't. In fact, it seemed to bring them closer together.

Lisa started working part-time for Philip in high school and was now considered a valuable member of the firm's enviable sales team. The team was considered an industry leader for its effectiveness - no doubt the result of Philip's tutelage.

At the time, Angela had been worried and talked to Philip about Lisa. Angela was surprised that Philip didn't know who she was. The crush Lisa had had on him was totally one sided. It made Angela feel a little sorry for Lisa and a little disgusted with Philip. However, it helped her feel a little more confident about her own relationship with him.

After the fight, Lisa had been apologetic and had actually sounded pleased for Angela. When Angela announced their engagement, Lisa desperately wanted to be part of the wedding party. Angela had been touched and pleased.

Angela shook her head and smiled, "Well, she's going to miss a great lunch."

Janet had to toss in her own comments, "Yeah, screw her. We can have a good time without her. I'll fill her in with the details later."

The other two chuckled, not at what she said, but more the way she said it. Lisa, however, was visibly disgusted with Janet. They had always been good friends, but Janet got on Lisa's nerves from time to time. This was one of those times. Lisa was about to say something when the waiter arrived. Lisa turned to him instead and ordered a double martini and a Chef's Salad. The waiter made a note on his pad and left. Lisa realized the other two had already ordered.

Lisa turned her attention again to Angela, "So where are you two going for your honeymoon. Somewhere fantastic no doubt," and she smiled.

Angela blushed, "Philip's got this great condo on the beach in St. Martin - on the Leeward side. I'm so looking forward to going there. It's going to be so romantic." She smiled openly at the thought of the time they were going to be spending in that fabulous part of the world.

Lisa's drink arrived and she immediately took a long sip. Angela detected a hint of jealousy in her manner, but dismissed it as innocent. She decided to proceed with the discussion of her plans for the big day and the roles these two would play.

* * * * *

There was a knock at the office door. The Lieutenant interrupted his briefing of Sam Davidson and looked to the door. "Okay, Sam. That's him." His gaze returned to Sam, he was serious - he was always serious. "Now remember, Sam. I want you to show him the ropes without your antics. I mean it!"

The Lieutenant was in his early fifties. He always wore dress slacks, and a white shirt and tie. Yet the shirt was always heavily wrinkled and the tie was never done to his neck. Dressed, he looked like an athlete. In his youth, a lifetime ago, he was. However, the years and the stresses of the job, had taken their toll. The bags under his gray eyes were the result of heavy smoking and the many sleepless nights his position demanded. His still full dark hair looked like a rat's nest. The Lieutenant had a habit of running his fingers through his hair when he was upset, nervous, or angry.

The Lieutenant had a strong personality and was very efficient even though he hated this desk job with its responsibilities and work load. He had much preferred working the streets and felt more alive being on the front lines. He had mentioned this fact to his long time friend, Sam, on many occasions. Sam had listened to his complaints many times, and although he respected his boss and the office he held, he enjoyed giving him a hard time. Sam was now looking at the mess of his hair, and the Lieutenant's fingers, once again, going through it. Lately, Sam had thought he had seen this man's hands on his head more often than on his desk.

Sam smiled back at his Lieutenant, it wasn't a comforting smile.

"I mean it Sam. It's his first day. Go easy on him."

Sam nodded, and spoke sarcastically, "No problem, chief."

The Lieutenant looked at him, disgusted, and raised his voice to the door, "Yeah. Come!"

Sam turned in his chair to face the door as his new partner entered. The Lieutenant had spent the last fifteen minutes briefing Sam on his new partner, so he knew all the facts about him, but, until this moment, they had only been words. Seeing him, Sam was struck by how young he looked - how cocky.

"He couldn't be more than thirty," Sam thought, as he looked him over quickly and completely. He was wearing blue jeans and tennis shoes, and on top, a denim shirt, a light brown sports coat, and what looked like a red denim tie. His hair was blonde and neat. It had to be, considering how short it was. Sam thought jokingly that Williams probably combed it with a towel.

Sam had been working solo ever since O'Brian took his golden handshake. Michael O'Brian had been the greatest possible partner. He could anticipate Sam's every move and Sam knew him equally as well. The two men had been more in tune with each other than the best of married couples. They had to be, everyday their lives depended on it.

Sam missed him, but had grown used to working alone. He almost liked it and now he was being assigned a new partner - a rookie at that. He knew Williams had been on the force for many years, but as a uniform. He had no experience as a detective.

The Lieutenant faked a smile as Williams strolled to the empty chair beside Sam, "Welcome. I'd like you to meet Sam Davidson. He will be your new partner."

Williams looked down at Sam and smiled broadly. The man he saw before him was easily in his mid fifties. His salt and pepper hair was neatly trimmed. His blue eyes looked somewhat cold. He was wearing a brown tweed sports coat which hung loosely over his white shirt and brown tie, a matching pair of brown slacks, and black shoes. Overall he looked neat and professional - but old. Williams was beginning to wonder if he was going to be babysitting and if the old man would be able to keep up with him.

William's voice held a hint of sarcasm with a touch of contempt which was almost camouflaged by sincerity, "I've been looking forward to meeting you. I've heard a lot about you. You're almost a legend around here. Sorry about your partner, but it worked out good for me, eh. It will be good to work with a master." He put on a broad smile and extended his hand to Sam.

Sam took it with an indignant smile, and used it to pull himself out of the chair. The force he used was almost enough to pull Williams off balance. Sam let out a theatrical grunt as he became erect. He gave a good impression of a dilapidated old man. Williams was caught off guard by it and looked towards the Lieutenant puzzled. The Lieutenant looked disgusted.

A touch of sincerity crept into Sam's expression. He let out a small chuckle, slapped Williams on the shoulder, and looked him in the eye, "Come on rookie. Let's smack your ass and towel you off. It's time for you to meet the world." He let out a belly laugh, and headed out of the Lieutenant's office.

The Lieutenant yelled after him, his voice didn't sound pleased, "Davidson!"

Sam didn't miss a step, chuckling as he went and motioning for Williams to follow. Williams shook his head and complied, realizing he had just been the brunt of some joke. He spoke sarcastically to no one in particular, "This is going to be so much fun."

Sam stopped when he reached his desk. He looked back at Williams and pointed to the desk just left of his own, "This is your desk."

Williams looked at it and then at Sam's. He could see they would be sitting face to face and wondered quickly if it would be possible to set them up another way. Just as quickly he shook it off, "I think I can handle this." He knew they hadn't started off very well. Williams had talked to the Lieutenant and had been told of Sam's habits and the like. He knew about O'Brian and felt an urge to try again. "Listen, Davidson. I know about O'Brian. I know how close you guys were. I'm sorry he retired, but I assure you I can do this. You'll see."

Sam looked at him and smiled. He thought, "You have no idea what this is all about. How can you possibly know whether or not you can do it?"

Sam looked to the pile of files neatly stacked on his desk and smiled. He took a number of the files off the top and slammed them down on William's desk. "Okay, Detective Williams, go through these. Bring yourself up to speed on them. We'll talk tomorrow. We'll see if you're a detective or not. I've got a few things to take care of. I'll see you bright and early in the morning. Be here at seven." Sam had no intention of arriving that early himself.

Williams looked at the stack of files that now sat on his desk and then back at Sam and nodded. He sat down and opened the top file, resisting the urge to lash out at his partner. Sam shouldn't be going anywhere right now, especially without him. The two of them should be going over these cases together, although he believed he would get more done if Sam wasn't here. He would stay quiet for now and let Sam leave.

Sam shook his head and left him to it. On his way out, Sam reviewed the last few minutes in his mind. It had all been a sort of test for his new partner and he had failed. William's hadn't tried to set Sam straight or defend himself. He had complied far too easily. How was Williams going to conduct insightful interviews with suspects and witnesses if he had missed what Sam had been trying to do? Sam shook his head again at the thought, "No independent thought - too compliant." He decided it was simply because Williams was a rookie. At least he hoped that was all it was.

After Sam had disappeared through the door, Williams thought, "That ass thinks he's pulling the wool over my eyes. I can see right through him. He's the master and I'm the green flunky. I'll show that SOB. I'm more than capable, I'm down right great. He'll see."

* * * * *

When Sam entered the dimly lit tavern he saw O'Brian sitting alone in a booth. As he sat down, O'Brian looked at him with a sinister smile, "You're late as usual." he paused for a moment then continued, "Well? Did you screw the poor boy over?"

Sam chuckled, "Ah, he's a rookie. I'm sure he'll be fine."

O'Brian shook his head as he took a sip of his beer. Sam looked to the bartender and held up a finger to place his order. His glance returned to O'Brian, and he thought how much older he looked. His hair, what hair he had left, was completely gray now. His face showed all the signs of age, with its deep crevices surrounded by plump hills of loose skin. His color was good though, healthy looking. Sam shook it off, he didn't want to think of his long time partner as old, "So, how's the fishing?"

O'Brian chuckled, "It's been great... I haven't caught a damn thing. I'm just so glad to be out of this sewer that it really doesn't matter." He smiled genuinely, "I go fishing. I tell Emily I'll bring home supper. I get home with no fish, and she's already got steak on the table." He shook his head, "She has such confidence in my abilities." and chuckled.

Sam knew how much O'Brian loved his wife. They had been married for almost forty years now. She had always been the one constant in his life, the anchor that kept him in place during all the storms this life had given him. Sam knew that if anything ever happened to her, O'Brian would be completely lost.

Sam had never gotten seriously involved with anyone. He always thought, "I'm a cop. It's more than what I do, it is who I am. Nothing is more important than the job." He knew that if there had been someone in his life, they would have to take second place to the work. He never wanted to subject anyone to that kind of life. But now, seeing O'Brian, and knowing the relationship he and his wife had, he started to realize that perhaps his beliefs were wrong. He thought of his own retirement not that far off and could imagine himself sitting in the dark all alone. He didn't like the image.

It was almost as if O'Brian had been reading his mind, "Emily says hi by the way. She's wondering when you are coming for dinner. She said that one of her girlfriends has a daughter she'd like you to..."

Sam interrupted him with his laughter. He knew what O'Brian was about to say and shook his head, "She's an incredible woman, your Emily - special. You're one lucky son of a bitch you old fart. How'd you manage to suck her in anyway?" Sam had heard the story of how O'Brian and his wife had gotten together all those years ago. The question was rhetorical and O'Brian knew it.

O'Brian half smiled and Sam could see his eyes glaze up slightly as he shook his head, his voice sounded serious, "I don't know. The god's must have been smiling on me that day" and took a long swill off his beer.

Sam saw it. It was clear, unmistakable love. He'd never seen it in O'Brian as clearly as he did at this very moment. He knew now he was going to have to get serious about trying to find a mate. What he saw in his partners face, the sound in his voice, he knew it was something he was missing. Something he no longer wanted to be without. He needed to feel like that for someone. It was after all, just a job.

7

Angela answered the phone before the third ring, "Hello?"

"Hello Angela. Dick... er... Richard Johnson here."

Angela's heart stopped. Her voice was controlled and she closed her eyes tightly, "Yes, Richard?"

Richard hesitated before continuing, "I'm afraid I haven't had much luck locating your father."

Angela's heart sank. Those were the very words she did not want to hear. Disappointment engulfed her.

Richard sounded remorseful, but sure, "I have found out a few things about him, though. Would you like to get together this afternoon?"

Angela's heart felt empty, but at least some information was better than nothing. She answered softly, "Yes, Richard. How about we meet at Jack's in an hour?"

"See you then," Richard replied.

Angela slowly replaced the receiver and stood for a moment, her hand resting on the phone. Her dream of having a father walk her down the aisle was gone. It had been a vision within her mind almost as strong as the image she had of the man she would be marrying. No words where strong enough to define the emptiness she now felt. A single tear escaped her eye as she started for the door.

* * * * *

Angela had just finished her second glass of wine when Richard came in. He scanned the restaurant as he entered. It was early and only four tables were occupied. Locating Angela quickly, he sat across from her. He noticed the empty wine glass in front of her, "A little early in the day for that, isn't it?"

She thought for a second, "Yes, you're probably right."

The waiter approached and Richard ordered, "Coffee, black, no sugar. Thanks," and looked across to Angela.

She held up her empty glass, "Another one of these, please."

The waiter nodded and left. Richard gave his head a quick shake. He was going to say something to her and thought better of it. It wasn't his place, "So tomorrow is the big day, eh?"

She smiled warmly and sounded a little distant. "How's Carol?"

The question surprised him, "Ah, she's fine, I guess. I'll let her know you were asking after her."

Angela acknowledged the reply with a nod, she really didn't care. While waiting for him, she had spent the time reviewing all that had happened during the last few weeks - all the last minute preparations for the wedding, all the relatives that had come to town for the event.

According to the teasing, it was to be the social event of the decade. She had been meticulous in planning to the smallest detail. However, the one thing she had wanted the most was not in the plan.

She tried to think of something other than herself, "Richard, you look different today." She looked him over studiously, "You know what it is?"

He shook his head. Angela continued, chuckling as she quickly scanned the restaurant, "It's like they say, the frame makes the picture," and she laughed.

Richard wasn't offended and laughed in return. "I don't get into these kinds of places very often." The restaurant appealed to him. A few more tables were now occupied and he believed the place would be full by lunch. He could imagine himself coming here again.

Angela nodded and continued, "Yes, tomorrow is the big day. Actually, we'll be having the reception right here." She paused for a second, "Did I tell you my lawyer is going to be giving me away?"

Richard didn't know how to respond to that. "How strange", he thought. He wasn't aware that her lawyer was also an old family friend. Angela had deliberately phrased the remark for maximum effect. The comment was made as punishment for his failure and judging by the expression on Richard's face, had achieved its purpose. However, seeing it didn't make her feel better.

Weeks ago Angela had asked Mr. Bonder if he would walk her down the aisle. She had hoped to be able to cancel him in favor of her own father. However, it was painfully obvious that that dream would not come true.

Richard reached into his jacket pocket and pulled out a small, nicely wrapped package, placed it on the table in front of Angela, and gestured for her to open it. She was genuinely surprised as she reached for it, "My goodness, what's this?"

"It's nothing really, just a little something for your wedding - a gift." He was a little embarrassed, and wondered if he should have bought it. She looked up at him with a very pleasant smile as she opened the package, wishing now that she hadn't made her earlier comment.

"Thank you, Richard. This is incredibly thoughtful of you."

Richard's smile held a hint of pride and he shrugged his shoulders, "It's nothing, really."

Inside the little box was a small crystal angel. In the light of the restaurant it sparkled brilliantly, looking as though it could come to life at any moment. Angela was thrilled and looked again into his eyes, "Thank you, Richard. Really, it's beautiful."

Richard smiled back, genuinely pleased, "I was walking by a small shop downtown and it caught my attention. I don't know why, it just reminded me of you and I knew I had to get it. I'm glad you like it."

Richard tried to make the gesture sound minimal. However, it was the first time in a very long time that he had felt the desire to purchase something special for anyone. "I hope all your wishes and dreams come true," he continued. He had read that somewhere.

Angela looked into his eyes, "That's very sweet, Richard. Thank you."

She played with the little figure for a few more seconds, then remembered why they were there and gently placed the angel back in its box.

She tried to sound pleasant and positive. "So Richard, you have a report for me?"

Richard nodded and pulled an envelope from his jacket pocket and handed it across the table. Angela promptly opened it. The waiter was back with their beverages before she had removed the contents.

Richard started, "What you will find in there," pointing to the envelope, "are the results of what I have uncovered."

He adjusted himself nervously in his chair and took a sip of his coffee.

"Mr. Simmons wasn't any kind of extraordinary guy. I'd say he was pretty average. He had a decent job, and made a decent living. A year after the date in the file you gave me, he met a woman. Wendy was her name - not that it matters. They dated for a couple of years and were married. A year after that, they bought their first house together. He worked and she stayed home. They didn't have any children." That single comment made Angela look up. She thought, "How ironic!" That was the only word to describe it - ironic.

Richard continued, "As best as I have been able to discover, their life was pretty uneventful for the first couple of years. Then about 15 years ago, his employer downsized and he was let go. It seems things took a nose dive after that. His pretty little wife had to go out to work. No big deal for most of us, but it tore him apart. Apparently, his one big fault was that he was a bit of a control freak. He had to have his wife chained to the house."

He thought about that comment a second, and wished he hadn't said it quite that way. He tried to rephrase it, "He felt he was supposed to be the bread winner, and his wife, the homemaker. Anyway, he wasn't able to find work. He didn't have any special skills. He hit the bottle - a little at first and then gradually, as is typical, pretty hard. One day he went out and never came back. He just vanished. No one had heard from him until about three years ago. Apparently, he had contacted his wife. She didn't want anything to do with him - wouldn't even talk to him. She wasn't of much help to me."

Angela was stunned, and thought, "Why is it that everybody treats my life so clinically?"

Richard saw the look on her face, "Sorry Angela, but that's all I could find." He had misread her expression.

She shook her head, "No, Richard, not at all. This is good." She paused for a second, "Not exactly what I had expected, let me tell you. I thought maybe he was married and living happily in another city with a brood of children or something. Certainly nothing like this."

Angela was deeply touched by Richard's report but didn't quite know what to make of it. She began to wonder whether her father was someone she really wanted to pursue or was it better that Richard hadn't been able to find him? She thought hard about it and decided she still needed and wanted to know him.

Richard smiled and continued seriously, "Believe me, Angela, the difference between a responsible upstanding person, and someone living in a gutter is a wall no thicker than a sheet of paper. A person can spend all their time building a life and one event, sometimes it can be something very small and seemingly insignificant but occurs entirely at the wrong time, and poof, he or she falls as far as a living person can fall." He paused, recounting his own situation. He was very somber, "Sometimes, if there is the desire, and the luck, a person can find their way back."

Richard thought of all the people he had known that never made it back. "Most people don't understand unless they have actually been there. Life is an illusion you know? People work hard, surround themselves with brick walls, and feel safe and secure, not realizing that the walls are really crepe paper and any strong wind can rip them apart."

Angela just stared at him. She felt compassion, grief, and pity for him now. Seeing the pain in his eyes she knew he was speaking from experience. She thought, "The horrors those eyes have witnessed - lived."

Richard was feeling a little embarrassed by drifting so far off topic. "Unprofessional," he thought and continued. "I've talked to his ex-wife, his ex-boss, neighbors, and even the mailman - anyone I could think of. No one seems to know what happened to him after that. There is an old photo in there that his ex-wife gave me. I did tell her about you. She thought you might like it."

Angela hadn't seen it yet, but looked at Richard and smiled. She was thrilled. "Maybe I should meet with her. Talk to her about him."

Richard frowned and thought carefully. He didn't want to hurt Angela but she had to know, "No. I asked her exactly that when I was talking to her. She has rebuilt her life but is still quite bitter about the whole thing with him. She was insistent about not wanting to meet you. I'm sorry Angela."

She was clearly upset but spoke thoughtfully, "No, Richard. I'm fine. I understand. Really I do. I'm sure I'd feel the same way."

Angela took a sip of her wine, "So where do we go from here?"

Richard looked confused, "Go from here? I told you I haven't been able to find a trail, nothing. He has vanished." As far as Richard was concerned the search was over.

Angela understood his expression and became assertive. "This isn't over!" Angela fumed, "you haven't found anything that says he's dead! I still want you to find him!"

Richard became annoyed, "That's true, I haven't found anything that says he is dead. I also haven't found anything that says he is still alive, either. This trail is cold. He's gone."

Angela was quiet for a few seconds, reflecting. Then she reached into the purse hanging on the back of her chair and pulled out an envelope. She held its bulk in her hands for a second then handed it across the table to Richard. She had planned on giving it to him today. It was supposed to be for him to continue his work. It hadn't occurred to her that he would be thinking of quitting. While he was opening it, she took another sip of her wine and watched the expression on his face.

Richard was shocked at the sight of all those hundred dollar bills. He put it on the table and looked at Angela, "Where does someone so young get this kind of money?" He looked around to make sure no one else had seen what was in the envelope. Satisfied no one had, he looked back at Angela. "That is one piss pot full of money, Angela."

Angela put down her glass, "Yes, Richard, it is."

She teased the wine glass with her fingers, thinking how best to say what she wanted to say. "I have spent twenty thousand dollars so far. That was just for the file I gave to you. I am not accustomed to just throwing money away. I expect something for it. You have done a great job for me so far." She paused briefly, "Deep down in my heart, I know he is still alive. Don't ask how, I just know, and since he is alive, he can be found. I believe very strongly that you are the man that can find him." She pointed to the envelope, "That should cover your expenses to date, and for sometime to come. There is more. My dad set up an account for me before he died. The money he put in it was for a dowry of sorts or something," she chuckled to herself, "I think he must have been a bit old fashioned. Anyway, it has grown into a tidy sum now. Believe me, I will spend every penny of it to find my father. Do you understand? I trust you and I trust your abilities, Richard."

Richard looked at Angela for almost a minute before he spoke. He knew she was the kind of person that was used to getting whatever she wanted. "I'm happy to take your money. God knows I could use it," he thought to himself for a second before continuing. "I'll keep looking. I'll do the best I can. Are you sure, Angela?"

Angela nodded and he put the envelope in his jacket pocket. Richard now felt an obligation to do his absolute best to find her father, but he felt in his heart it was unlikely he would be successful. Still he wanted to try for her. He wanted to continue for her. He sincerely wanted to find this man for her - and himself.

Richard stood without saying another word and smiled at her as he left. Angela convinced herself that the meeting had gone well. Richard would continue the search and she hoped he really would give it his best effort.

She looked at her watch. It confirmed what her body was saying, it was lunch time. She ordered something to eat. Taking another sip of her wine she looked at the envelope he had given her. She picked it up and fumbled with it for a few seconds, then pulled out the contents. Inside were a number of neatly typed pages. Richard had given an excellent summation in their conversation.

Attached to the back page was the photograph he had mentioned. She thought how utterly impersonal it looked. She took the photograph and stared at it. She thought the man it portrayed was handsome. Of course he would be. He was her father. He was slight of build and looked to be in reasonably good shape. She could see many of her own features in his face. She looked into the eyes, trying to see his soul but it was just a photograph. Her face showed the torment within her. She wanted to cry now, but couldn't.

For months and years she had been referring to this unknown man as father. She had never met him. He had never had a name, or a face, or anything that could be considered tangible in anyway. In reality, he was simply a sperm donor. An anonymous faceless male that donated the DNA, that in part had created her. She could refer to him as sperm donor, or Affero Vita, or some other non-titled name, but none of those were appropriate to her. Referring to him as anything less than father would only serve to minimize herself as a person, and that was simply unacceptable.

Her dad had raised her and had been the husband of her mother. That man was real and she loved him as much as she was able - as much as any daughter could love their dad. The image of the man before her now had a face and a name, he was her father. To her, he was the man that gave her life. He was the other half of the reproductive equation and she had no difficulty in making the distinction between the two men. Her dad was her dad and nothing would ever change that. This man was her father and nothing could ever change that.

8

The house was buzzing with the sounds of laughter. The bridesmaids were fluttering around, faces aglow, getting themselves ready. They knew everyone would be looking at them and they wanted their appearance to be perfect.

Angela stood calmly in front of a full length mirror looking radiant in her long white gown. Elaine and Janet moved around her ensuring everything was just right. The two of them talked while busily performing their tasks, completely ignoring the woman wearing the gown.

Angela wasn't listening to them anyway. She was focused on memories of her childhood, and of her teenage years, and of the years that passed after that. She replayed all those years; they were a path leading to this day.

She thought of Philip and the times they had shared and the plans they had made. She thought about the things in her life that were about to end and the new things that were about to begin. She was truly in love with Philip, and was sure of his love for her. There was no doubt in her mind that she was doing the right thing. Nothing else mattered to her today. It was her special day. The fairy tale she had dreamed of since she was a small girl.

"It's almost time, dear. Are you ready?" It was the first time in almost an hour that Elaine had talked directly to her daughter.

Angela looked into her mother's eyes, sharing her most beautiful smile and simply nodded.

Janet stood back to get a full view of the vision in the gown. "Damn, girl, you look good enough to eat."

Angela was a little annoyed by Janet's comment. She wasn't angry, but just wished that today Janet could be a little different - a little less Janet.

Simon was downstairs pacing, looking at his watch, and wondering what exactly the women were doing up there that was taking so long. He wanted to be doing something - he needed to be doing something. He was as nervous as if he were the father of the bride. All he had to do was escort Angela down the aisle, but to Simon it was a very significant role, and he felt it a great honor to be "giving Angela away". He believed at this moment that it was the greatest role he had ever been asked to perform. He felt as though he were a member of the family and there was great pride in that thought.

Simon could hear the women giggling and laughing, and was a little annoyed by it. They should be more serious; he couldn't understand the woman's perspective on weddings.

The photographer was standing by a table nibbling at the food that had been laid out. Simon turned to look up the stairs and spoke out loud, "Here she comes." Hearing him, the photographer wiped his hands on his pants and readied his camera.

Simon smiled broadly - how beautiful Angela looked descending the stairs. She moved with such poise and grace. He felt proud and wasn't sure why. He approached her as she reached the base of the stairs and took her face gently in both of his hands giving her a soft kiss on the forehead.

His voice was gentle, inaudible to anyone except her, "You look positively beautiful, Angela. He is one very lucky man. I hope he realizes how lucky he is."

She beamed back at Simon and took his arm as they turned to face the photographer. The bridesmaids gathered around standing at different levels on the staircase. The strobe from the camera went off, filling the room with an instant of bright light, then again and again, capturing each pose.

Between each shot, Simon looked at his watch, and his anxiety grew. As they were finally getting into the limousine, Simon remarked, "You know Angela, we're going be late." He was genuinely worried. He didn't like the thought of tardiness for such an important event.

Angela looked at him and giggled. The look on her face was trying to say, “Of course we are. We're supposed to be.”

Elaine looked at him and gave him a warm smile. She leaned forward and gave him a light kiss on his cheek, "You know Simon, sometimes you can be so cute."

Simon was confused, but dismissed it as a female thing.

* * * * *

Philip was visibly nervous as he stood at the front of the church. He checked his watch continuously and began to think that Angela had changed her mind and wouldn't be coming. Then he realized it was intentional as he remembered that it was part of the wedding ritual - make the groom sweat. “A stupid tradition,” he thought. He stared back at the door in anticipation. He was unaware of all the people that filled the church - his family and relatives, and her relatives and friends. All those eyes were on him and he didn't notice.

Finally, the large doors opened and the organ began to play. One by one the bridesmaids and escorts entered the church, and proceeded slowly up the aisle. There was definite relief on Philip's face as each entered and made their way forward. Each smiled so beautifully and glanced proudly back and forth across the crowd as they advanced. The congregation looked politely at each but they were waiting for Angela's entrance.

Then Angela appeared in the doorway. She focused on the front of the church, waiting patiently for all the bridesmaids to take their places. She was glowing with an air of purity. She could see Philip standing at the front waiting for her with his hands clasped in front of himself. She thought how handsome he looked and how completely nervous he was. She was pleased by that, believing he wouldn't be nervous if he didn't really care.

Mike leaned in to Philip and whispered, "It's not too late, Bud. You can back out and I'll take over for you."

Philip glared at him, "Best man in title only, buddy", and drove his elbow gently into Mike's ribs. His eyes returned to Angela.

Simon looked proud and distinguished as he joined Angela. They began their procession slowly up the aisle, bathed in an endless sea of camera flashes and the hum of whispers. All were pointing at Angela approvingly. It was exactly how Angela had envisioned it and she was very content.

Angela's eyes didn't move from her intended destination. Still, she was fully aware of everyone in the pews. Her peripheral vision recognized many of the faces she had hoped would be here. She recorded in her mind everything - the people, the looks on their faces, the sounds of the organ, how she walked, the look on Philip's face - everything. She wanted to ensure she remembered it all. They would be memories she would recall later, and for the rest of her life. She wanted them to be complete.

Watching Angela's progress, Philip's nervousness disappeared. As he gazed at her, his heart felt warm. She looked more like an angel than a human being. At this moment, he was sure that nothing had ever been so right. He felt very lucky, very happy, and very much in love.

Angela stopped as she passed the first pew and turned to Simon. His face was lit by a proud smile, and she was glad he had agreed to be here for her. He had been everything she had wanted him to be. He reached forward and lifted the veil that covered her face and gave her a small kiss on her forehead. "I'm so happy for you, dear", he said.

Angela was surprised by those words. He had never said "Dear", quite that way before. The sound of it touched her deeply, and she smiled warmly. He sat and took Elaine's hand in his and smiled as Angela took her place beside Philip. Angela handed her bouquet to Janet and smiled as she turned to Philip. She noticed his eyes were glazed over with moisture and the sight of them sent a rush of warmth through her body. They both turned to the minister. Every step had been designed for effect and rehearsed for accuracy, but yet had been so natural. The minister began, "Dearly beloved..."

* * * * *

Angela had been surprised when the owner of Jack's had approached her all those months ago. He had offered Angela the use of the restaurant for her reception saying it was his gift to her. He knew how much the restaurant had come to mean to Angela, her family, and her friends. He was grateful for the support they had given his business over the years and this was one thing he could do for her in return.

Angela had been touched by the offer, saying she couldn't imagine a more fitting setting to celebrate her marriage. Since it was the place that was so special to her, she insisted on paying for the food and beverages. The owner flatly refused - the entire reception was to be his gift.

All the tables were topped with white linen tablecloths and set with fine china. In the middle of each table, a candle glowed in a bed of flowers. The irresistible magic of the fairy lights on the patio drew many guests outside to hear the sound of the sea playing a symphony as it rushed to shore. Even the sky seemed to have added extra stars for this night. Standing on the deck, listening to the strings playing in the background, one knew that something special had happened.

Philip had been the typical male throughout the planning. He had wanted to support Angela and help with the plans, and indeed, had tried. However, he knew that for this day at least, he was only marginally more than a supporting actor in the performance. Angela had asked his opinion on many occasions, and he had given it without hesitation, but was usually wrong. It could have made him angry, but it didn't. He knew his place, understood his role, and tried to live up to her vision. But even at that, he had made the comment, "Well, Angela, why don't you just tell me what I think and then I'll know what to say." Hearing those words, she would just laugh and carry on. None of it had bothered him - it had always been that way and that way it would always be.

* * * * *

Philip had gone down early to the patio, not wanting to wake Angela. She had looked so beautiful in her sleep and he couldn't bring himself to disturb her. Now she lay awake, looking up at the ceiling with a contented smile on her face.

The Caribbean morning sun poured through the window of the room and across the bed as Angela reviewed every minute of the wedding. The memories she had so carefully recorded in her mind, she now replayed. She recalled every syllable of their vows and relived the joy she felt as she and Philip cut the cake. She remembered the guests laughing, talking, drinking, and dancing. The speech Simon made had been inspiring. She saw her mother and Simon dancing all night and thought how perfectly natural they seemed together.

Angela laughed to herself when she thought about Janet and Mike, and how they had enjoyed the entire evening together. She remembered the surprise and joy on Janet's face when she caught the bouquet and the terror in Mike's eyes when her garter landed on his head.

Philip sat quietly on the patio, sipping his coffee and staring aimlessly out to sea. The wedding had been such a blur to him. He wasn't entirely sure who all had been there. He remembered seeing a few friends and family there, and he recalled how Angela looked as she came down the aisle. All other details he could only remember as having been nice. He now hoped the photographs would turn out - he would need them to rebuild his memory. He knew Angela had been very pleased and to him that was all that really mattered.

Sea birds drifted by on the wind, and for a second he thought he could join them. Teal blue fingers tipped in white reached towards him across the sand. Roaring, as if vocalizing their displeasure at being unable to touch him - they retreated and tried again. The sound was mesmerizing, calming. Further out he could see boats rising and falling on the waves and diamonds of light glistened off the crystal clear water. He thought to himself how this must be the most perfect place on Earth. Then he thought of Angela. "I should go get her so she can enjoy this with me." He took another sip of his coffee. "I'll go in a minute," he thought, and sank deeper into his chair.

Angela walked out onto the patio and saw Philip sitting there. She walked up to him casually from behind, bent forward, and put her hands on his shoulders. She kissed him on the top of his head and spoke so softly, "Here you are?"

She smiled sweetly and sat down beside him. Last night came rushing back to her. How gently he had held her. How sweetly he had loved her. She was sure in her own mind that no one else in the world had ever experienced as wonderful a first night as they had.

"Good morning," Philip said. The gentle touch of Angela's lips on his head had brought his focus back to this place. "Did you sleep well?"

She looked at him and smiled. Her face was that of a little girl with a secret she wanted to tell the whole world.

"I was just about to come up and get you. It's truly beautiful out here this morning," Philip continued.

She remembered how he had looked when she had walked out onto the patio. He looked so comfortable and deep in thought. She knew that there was no way he was coming up to her. She smiled. It was a fib and she didn't care.

Angela turned her gaze to the ocean and brushed her hair aside. They sat for some time in silence. The sea worked its magic, drawing them both deep within its spell. Sunbathers began to claim their territory on the sand. The peaceful harmony of nature was being overpowered by the hum of human activity. Angela and Philip looked at each other and without exchanging a word they retreated inside and back up to the bedroom. The rest of the world would have to wait.

* * * * *

Their week had passed far too quickly. The days had been filled with hand in hand walks on the sand; their evenings spent dining by candle light. Romance, passion and love were the spices that seasoned their days. It was a fairy tale from her childhood. Inevitably, reality would take over and neither of them welcomed the thought of returning home.

9

Philip had already gone to the office. Sitting in her housecoat, drinking her tea, Angela thought about what he has said, "Do anything you want to the place – it's your home now." Philip knew Angela wouldn't be happy with this house as it was. She would have to make her mark on it which would change this house into their home.

The house had been a prestigious address Philip had acquired to impress business associates and prospects, and a place to sleep. Although he had spent much time choosing the style and the architectural details of the building, for him it didn't have any significance beyond that.

Women need the comfort and security of a stable nest but Philip knew men didn't feel that need to the same degree. He believed that a house is only a house until a woman puts her touches on it. Then and only then is it transformed into the warmest and most comfortable place on earth.

Angela was looking forward to the task ahead as she wandered contentedly around her new home sipping a fresh cup of Earl Gray. With a satisfied smile, she began to plan. As a girl in her mother's home she had often redone her own room, and that space had gone through a great many incarnations. Now, she was a married woman. In this house, she and Philip would live their lives, entertain their friends and associates, and eventually raise a family. She needed their home to accommodate all those functions. Their surroundings absolutely had to be fun, as well as conservative, formal, and functional. She knew it was going to be a challenge, but it was also going to be a most enjoyable undertaking.

Although she had been in this house many times, and had planned what she would do, things now looked different. Now it was her home, and she was seeing it as if for the first time.

Soon the living room coffee table was covered with designer magazines. Photographs were cut out and stacked in specific piles. She took the photographs and wandered through each room in turn, trying to visualize the effects of each design. She peered through each window to experience the view offered and to see how the light played off the walls and corners. She imagined the colours, the feel, the smell, and the touch of each room. She tried to let each room tell her what it wanted to be.

Through it all, the smile never left her face. She felt warm inside, and truly happy. She knew it would be days before she purchased as much as a can of paint. Angela wanted to be absolutely sure of everything before she started.

It had been a full morning. She sat on the couch, cup of tea in hand. She had considered using a professional decorator to do the work, but was glad she had decided against it. This job was going to be far too pleasant to give away to someone else.

The ringing phone startled Angela.

"So girlfriend, how was it? I wanna hear all about it." Angela glanced at the clock and thought to herself, "Twelve thirty, where did the morning go?"

Angela knew precisely what Janet was talking about. "It was perfect, Janet, absolutely perfect."

"You gotta tell me everything. Every juicy detail," Janet giggled. "How 'bout lunch?"

Angela shook her head. "Janet," she started to say something and changed her mind. A diversion would probably be a good idea. "Sounds good. See you in an hour?"

"Love ya." was Janet's response as each hung up.

* * * * *

They were sitting in Jack's talking and giggling. Their eyes wide and bright, looking and sounding like schoolgirls sharing their secrets.

Their meals and half a bottle of wine were gone as Angela completed her tale of the honeymoon. She had lived up to her obligatory end of the feminine ritual. She had told her everything. Angela had conveyed enough information so that Janet could easily have pictured herself there. Her duty done, Angela turned to Janet, "So, your turn... Mike?"

"Mike's Mike." Janet started with the smile of a child who had just been caught sneaking a treat. Janet was searching her mind, trying to decide how much information she wanted to share. She realized that she needed and wanted to tell everything. In fact, she had been waiting for Angela to return so she could share her news. She began.

"We've seen each other everyday since you've been gone", she giggled, "I had no idea he could be so charming."

Angela thought, "Charming! Mike?" That was one word she never thought anyone would ever use to describe Mike. Janet saw the sudden surprise on Angela's face and she giggled as she tilted her head shyly, "Well, maybe charming is a little strong." They both laughed.

"He's incredible in the sack though, like a man possessed or something." She laughed again.

Angela was satisfied, that sounded more like Janet. She wasn't sure in her own mind if that description was a good thing or not but she knew it was exactly the kind of thing Janet liked. "Serious?" Angela continued.

Janet thought for a second before she replied, "You know me. I'm not too serious about anything, but yeah, maybe. I've seen a side of him I hadn't seen before." Janet paused. "I don't know, maybe it's just the sex." She laughed again. Angela was smiling and shaking her head.

Janet knew it was more than that. The feelings she had for Mike were unlike anything she had felt before. It was real, and she knew Mike felt the same way. But, she was determined to live up to her reputation as the spinny blonde chick, even with her best friend. It was her protection from the world and because of it, people never expected too much from her. She listened to all the blonde jokes and always laughed along. She heard how people talked about her behind her back and encouraged it. It just made life so much easier and prevented anyone or anything from getting close enough to hurt her.

She believed that everyone carried a shield of some kind. Some hid behind the bottle, some used anger, and some would dress in the finest clothes to appear superior. Everyone had their own way, and the spinny blonde chick was hers. It gave her the protection she needed and still allowed her to have fun and to enjoy the things she wanted in life.

Janet and Mike had known each other much longer than Angela and Philip. They had never really been interested in each other before. "Too similar," Angela had often thought. They both had good hearts but both were very abrasive.

Most people could handle them in small doses only - everyone that is, except Angela and Philip;

however, they had always been able to see the inner depth of their respective friends. It was that inner soul that had kept them all as friends. Looking at Janet now, Angela thought how funny it was that weddings seem to bring the most unlikely people together. She chuckled to herself realizing it hadn't been just her special day. It had meant different things to each person that had been there, many of which she would never know.

Janet continued the story of her relationship with Mike. Angela was a little disgusted by some of the images Janet created. However, there was something about the stories that made Angela want to hear more. She could see the look in Janet's eyes and the way she held herself. She could see that Janet was falling in love and she felt happy for her.

When Janet had finished, Angela giggled. "Well Janet. After that I think I need a cigarette." Both women laughed.

Janet changed the subject. "So tell me, Ange. Are you going back to work?"

Angela thought about the question for a few seconds, "I don't know. Philip and I talked about it." She paused and smiled, "Well, I talked about it, he listened." They both laughed. "But seriously, I don't know if I want to. Philip's, Philip. I mean, he doesn't care one way or the other." she hesitated, "He's right, we certainly don't need the money, but I really enjoyed what I was doing. It was very satisfying. I know Mom really enjoyed having me around all the time. On the other hand, we are starting our lives together, we want some kids. It's kind of a romantic notion to stay at home and let my man take care of me." She paused at that. Reflecting on the many daydreams she had had about what she wanted from life. There was no reason why she shouldn't have it all.

"His hou... our house could definitely use a woman's touch." She giggled again, and continued confidently. "It is a beautiful place. I have given it a lot of thought and I know what I want to do. It's going to take a lot of work, but I know it is going to be fun."

Janet laughed knowingly at that. She had been in Philip's house many times, and although she liked it, had often thought there was something missing. Now she knew what it was - Angela. She knew her friend would change the whole feel of the place and she knew it would be spectacular.

"Well, Ange. It sounds to me like you have made up your mind," Janet said and laughed. "You'll be staying home, and taking me out for lunches."

The two visited for the rest of the afternoon. This time and place, for now, was the only thing that mattered. They sat telling stories and enjoying each other's company. Angela was going to make a point of doing this more often. It was good for the soul, she thought.

10

Elaine opened the door and returned Angela's smile as she hugged her warmly. Angela had been over almost every other day during the month since her wedding. Neither of them had as yet grown accustomed to Angela not living in this house. For Angela, ringing the doorbell was especially difficult. Although she knew it wasn't necessary, she felt it was more appropriate now that she was a guest and not a resident.

They sat beside each other on the couch as a pleasant fire crackled in front of them. Elaine had her silver tea service and best china cups arranged on the coffee table. Angela had always liked this service. It had been given to Elaine by her mother, and Angela knew in time, it would be hers.

Her mother had always reserved this set for special visitors. Seeing it there made Angela uncomfortable - she felt a little like a stranger. She would much have preferred the kitchen mugs the two normally used when they visited together. She was about to comment on just that when Elaine spoke.

"So where's our Philip off to this time?" Elaine asked as she poured the tea.

Angela smiled, disappointed she had missed her opportunity. "Later," she thought. "East Coast, I believe. Someone new, I think. I'm really not sure. He doesn't like to talk about business much."

Elaine smiled and handed Angela a cup of tea. Elaine also believed that work was work. When she was at work, she was totally focused. When she wasn't, work was the last thing she wanted to think about.

Angela had heard all the clichés: "work is work; never mix work with pleasure, etc. etc." However, Angela knew the reality - her mother thought about work all the time, even when she was sleeping she was at work! Philip was the same and it bothered Angela that he didn't share that part of his life with her.

"Is he going to be away long, this time?" Elaine picked up her cup, and took a sip of the sweet, hot liquid.

Angela shrugged her shoulders, "He said it was only going to be a few days," she chuckled. "He's funny. He always complains about going on these trips, but I know he just loves it. I mean smoozing a prospect was what made him. He's very good at it."

Elaine smiled, "He can be very charming when he wants to be," she said. She took a sip of her tea and asked, "When do you think you will be coming back to work, Angela?"

Angela hesitated before answering, "I've been thinking about that a lot lately. I really do miss all the excitement - even the stress." She paused, reflecting. "I'm having a great time right now. Doing our house is so much fun - the planning, the shopping, all of it. I see Janet almost everyday for lunch. I'm always there when Philip gets home, and we spend the evenings together." She paused for a second, shook her head, and took another sip of her tea. "I'm sure the novelty will wear off soon enough. Then I'll probably come banging on your door." She laughed at that, "If you'll have me back, that is."

Elaine smiled, politely. "You'll always have a job waiting for you, you know that. I had always hoped that when I retired, you would take over."

Elaine's dream had been for Angela to take over the business she and her husband had started. It was their legacy. However, deep in her heart she knew that, although Angela was good at business, running a company just wasn't her forte. When the day came for Elaine to retire, she would probably just sell out and have someone else take over. In fact, she already had someone in mind.

Retirement, for Elaine, wasn't far away. She was already feeling tired and thinking of the many things she still wanted to see and do. She had all the security she could ever possibly need, and Angela was grown and married. It was time to think about giving it all up and really start living. However, she wasn't quite to the point of telling Angela yet, not quite.

Angela smiled politely, "I'd like that". Although she enjoyed the business and liked interacting with customers, Angela wasn't sure she was willing to dedicate herself so totally to something like a business the way her mother had. Elaine ran the company effortlessly, and was still always available for Angela. Angela didn't believe she could do that or that she even wanted to. However, she had plenty of time before a decision had to be made - and things change.

Angela took a sip of her tea before continuing, "So Mom, any luck finding an apartment?"

Elaine perked up, "Well yes, I did. It's a really cute place downtown, only a few blocks from the office." She paused, remembering the fun she had had looking and planning and finally finding the perfect place. "It's on the tenth floor with a great view of the river and the park. It is a little small, only about twenty five hundred square feet, but really charming with hardwood floors, a fireplace, plus two bedrooms and a den. I take possession at the end of the month. I am very excited. I can hardly wait for you to see it, dear."

Angela was smiling and nodded her head. It felt good to see her mother so happy. She believed that if her mother were to continue living in this house alone, she would eventually get swallowed up by loneliness and depression, especially after she retired.

"When I first started looking, I thought I would like to move things from here to the new place, but I think I'm going to decorate it from scratch. I will, of course, take some of my special treasures, but I thought it would be exciting to make it totally different from this place. You know what I mean?"

"I'm sorry I didn't get a chance to help you look, Mom. I think it would have been fun." Angela said sadly.

Elaine smiled and replied, "I'm sorry too dear, but I know how busy you have been for the last few weeks."

Angela's own experiences had shown her how enjoyable decorating could be. She had kidded that she would like to have several homes, each done up differently. It would be fun to do, and it would make each uniquely special. "You'll have to let me help decorate. I've come across some really quaint shops. I've been having a great time doing our place. I think it would be a lot of fun - the two of us working side by side."

Elaine nodded, "I think that would wonderful. I could use your expertise." Elaine was quite capable on her own, but she loved to have Angela around and this would be one way to accomplish that. She missed not seeing her daughter's face every day.

The phone rang and Elaine picked it up, "Hello."

Elaine was a little confused, "Why, yes, she is," and handed the phone to Angela.

Angela took the phone from her mother's hand, "Who would be phoning me here?" she thought, "Hello?"

"Hi, Angela. Richard Johnson. I tried your number but you weren't there. I took a chance that you might be at your mother's." He paused for a second and when he started to talk again his voice cracked, "I found him!"

Angela was stunned. She was glad she was sitting down - she surely would have fainted if she hadn't been. She looked up at her mother and a single tear rolled down her cheek. The words echoed in her head, "I found him!" over and over, "I found him!" Angela reached for her mother's hand.

* * * * *

Angela and Elaine sat in silence. The room was full of faces and a steady drone of conversation, yet they felt completely alone - isolated.

Unnoticed, the waiter brought the coffees they had ordered. Their focus was fixated with anticipation on the front door of the restaurant. They were waiting for their past and their future to arrive.

Richard breezed in beaming. He knew Angela's life was about to change forever and he was pleased that he had accomplished a very good thing.

As he reached the table he looked at Elaine. Angela began, her voice was guarded and polite, "Richard. Hello. This is my mother, Elaine."

He offered his hand, "Hello, Mrs. Michails. I'm Richard Johnson. I'm very pleased to meet you." He recognized her from the wedding but they hadn't been formally introduced.

Elaine took his hand, "Mr. Johnson, pleasure. Angela has told me all about you", and she smiled politely.

He sat across from them, still beaming. "Well, I hope she didn't tell you everything." He meant it as a joke and laughed. The ladies responded with polite laughter of their own.

From his jacket pocket, Richard pulled an envelope. Using both hands, he gently placed the envelope in front of Angela, handling it as if it were the very finest of crystal.

Angela and Elaine sat looking at it as Richard ordered himself a coffee. The coffee arrived and still the two women were staring at the envelope. Richard was surprised. He had thought that they would have torn the package open immediately.

"Well, aren't you going to open it?" he said, still excited. He had wanted to make Angela happy and was almost disappointed by their apparent lack of enthusiasm.

Angela looked up at him and smiled. "Of course, Richard. We're just a little stunned. We were convinced this day would never come." Then she looked over at her mother. "We're not really sure how to react." Angela reached for the envelope and Elaine put her hand on top of Angela's, stopping her. She looked deep into her daughter's eyes, "Are you sure, dear. I mean, really sure."

Angela paused for a couple of seconds and thought, "Once you know a thing, there is no way you can ever not know it." Angela nodded her head and smiled. Her mother pulled her hand back slowly and closed her eyes as Angela opened the manila envelope and pulled out its contents. Staring back at her were several photographs. They were obviously recent and of the man in the previous photo - only older. She was pleased by the image she saw. The candid shots were taken of him at work. He looked good in a white shirt and tie. Angela flipped through the pictures one by one, glancing up at Richard between each. He was still beaming proudly.

Attached to the last photograph were several neatly typed pages and on the top of each page was the letterhead - Richard Johnson, PI.

Angela looked at Richard, "You changed the name?"

He smiled as he shrugged his shoulders, "I've moved my office, too," and he pointed to the address typed below the name. She recognized it as a much better part of town; obviously he was trying to attract a better clientele. Angela felt a touch of pride thinking she might have had something to do with that.

Angela started to read. It was all there - his name, and a current address and phone number. There was also a complete report, but Richard couldn't wait and spoke before she could read further.

"Apparently he was one of the lucky ones", he looked thoughtfully at both Elaine and Angela. His voice made Elaine's eyes open again, but she remained quiet.

"He found a way back. He's still in town. That's probably the only reason I was able to find him. When he disappeared, he was living on the streets – a bum. He slept in cardboard boxes - his days filled with trying to find his next drink. He took his meals, what meals he had, at the soup kitchen. He was very much one of the forgotten many."

He looked at Elaine again. Her pain was obvious so he decided to skip many of the details - it was all in the report anyway. "At the shelter, one of the staff took him under her wing. After several weeks, she was able to help him to convince himself to get the help he needed."

He paused, reflecting, "That's really what does it, you know. You have to convince yourself." He shook his head.

"Anyway, it was a long process with many regressions before he was back. The organization that provided help continued to work with him through it all – they even helped him find a job at a local hotel. It's not the greatest job, but it's good, honest work. He's been there for the last four years. His apartment is close so he walks to work. He's really getting himself back on track." Richard sounded proud of him - as if he was a kindred spirit.

Elaine searched for feelings in her daughter's eyes. Angela returned her mother's gaze, her eyes were wet and she was smiling. "We've found him" and she giggled. Elaine smiled back politely and nodded.

Angela looked at Richard, "It sounds like you actually talked to him. What's he like?"

Richard was about to taste his coffee but instead put the cup down and looked at Elaine instead of Angela. "Yes, I did. I wasn't sure if I should, but yeah, we had a nice chat. He's very nice - very pleasant. He is pretty impressive considering his little trip through hell."

Angela was serious, cautious, and scared, "Did you tell him about me?"

Richard smiled again, nodding, "I did. He wants very much to meet you. I think he is looking for a connection, now that he has made it through."

He pointed to the papers still in Angela's hands, "He doesn't have a phone of his own, but gave a number where he can be reached." Richard's tone became serious, "Angela, please don't just arrive on his doorstep. Make the first contact by phone. Talk first. Listen to him. If you feel right, then go from there. You are very different people. Know for sure, before you pursue this any further. Take one step at a time. Go slow - Promise me."

Angela understood what he meant, and nodded, "Thank you, Richard. I promise."

He looked at Elaine again. "Listen, you girls have things to talk about. I'm going to take off." He looked over at Angela; his voice was sincere, "If you need me for anything, call. Okay? I mean it. Anything!"

She nodded again, "Thank you so much for everything."

He started to get up but hesitated. He reached into his pocket, "I almost forgot." He pulled out another envelope, and handed it towards Angela, "Your change. I didn't need it all," and he smiled at her. Angela was both surprised and pleased by the gesture but put up her hand to stop him. "No Richard, please keep it. You have most definitely earned it."

He hesitated, looking into her eyes, then smiled and returned it to his pocket. "Angela, you are a very special woman. It has been a rare privilege to have met you. You have touched me deeply. Please take very special care of yourself." Turning to Elaine he said, "You must be very proud of your daughter."

Elaine noted the caution he was trying to hide, then looking back at Angela, she replied, "I am - very proud indeed. Thank you." It was the first thing she was sure of since he had sat down at the table. Richard smiled politely and left.

"Well, he certainly sounds pleased with himself," Elaine started.

Angela was surprised by her mother's cynical tone. Her response was equally short, "He knew how much I wanted this, Mom."

"Of course dear," she was guarded and pointed to the papers Angela was holding, "Please Angela, pay attention to what he said. Don't call this man. At least not right away. So much has happened. Don't react emotionally. Think this through very carefully."

Angela was stunned by her mother's words, "I thought you wanted to know about him, too? I have thought it through. I've dreamed of this day."

"Yes I know, dear. Really I do, but Richard is right. You're totally different people from two completely different worlds." Elaine took a sip of coffee and for a second wished that it was something stronger, "I just have a bad feeling about this, that's all."

11

Philip sat on the edge of the bed holding his head in his hands, staring at his feet. He thought, "My god, my head hurts. Why did I drink so much?" Something stirred behind him and he glanced over his shoulder and saw a young woman sleeping. He looked at her for a short moment then returned his head to his hands.

The previous night's activities were hazy. Philip remembered the all day meetings with Henry Ferguson. He liked Henry and believed they were going to have a great business relationship - maybe even a friendship. Henry loved to party, so after their meetings they went for dinner, and then on to Henry's favourite strip club.

Later, they went to a trendy dance club appropriately named 'The Sin Pit'. The music was too loud and the air was thick with the smoke from the pyrotechnics and cigarettes. The blend of a thousand perfumes, mixed with the aromas of alcohol and tobacco gave the place a pungent odor. Since every man and woman there seemed to be on the hunt it was easy pickings.

Philip glanced back at the woman in his bed and smiled, then looking around he realized this was neither his bed nor his room. He chuckled again and shook his head.

The woman woke up, rolled over, and looked at him sitting there. She smiled, "Morning lover."

Philip looked back at her and smiled, thinking how pretty she was. He got up and headed to the shower. He needed to freshen up but also hoped to find something that would identify this woman in the bed who somehow seemed familiar. His thoughts went to Angela, "This is the last time." He meant it, but in thinking of his wife he suddenly remembered where he had seen this woman before, "Oh my god, no! Lisa!"

* * * * *

Angela and her mother talked until three in the morning. "She didn't try to talk me out of it," Angela thought. She was just concerned trying to ensure that Angela had considered all the angles, scenarios, and possibilities. When Elaine was certain she had covered everything, she left Angela alone to think, trusting that she would do the right thing.

As dawn broke, Angela was still wearing the clothes from the day before. She sipped her tea and looked over the yard, remembering all the games she and her mother had invented there. She remembered all her birthday parties, her school days, her first date, and getting her driver's license. She remembered all the things her mother had helped her with and all the things for which her mother had scolded her.

Through all of these experiences, her mother had always been there to support and guide her. She giggled to think of all the antics her mother would have kept from Dad had he lived. Her thoughts then turned to the future which looked wonderful. "Do I really want to complicate it?" she wondered. "Complicate it? That was definitely not the right word." She thought. Meeting him would answer so many of her questions and make her feel complete. She was sure of her decision, "Today is the day!"

After a soothing bubble bath and a good breakfast she was ready. She picked up the phone, with her hands shaking, keyed in the number from Richard's report.

A pleasant female voice answered, "Good morning. Drake Hotel, Andrea speaking. How may I help you?"

Angela stood there in silence. Her heart was pounding so loudly she was sure it was going to beat its way out of her chest. She wanted to speak but the words just wouldn't form.

Andrea spoke again, "Hello?"

The sound of the voice again startled Angela and she quickly hung up. She stood silently, leaning on the phone. A million thoughts raced through her mind - past conversations with her mother and the previous night's talks. She had been obsessed with the search, but now the search was over. The dream had become the most important thing and now the dream was a reality. She was mourning its loss.

She remembered reading an article relating to human nature and wealth building. The study examined people who claimed they wanted to be financially wealthy, yet practiced extremely bad money management habits. Subconsciously, the dream was more important than achieving the goal. Angela suddenly felt silly. "That's what I'm doing," she thought, and dialed the number again.

The same voice answered, "Good morning, Drake Hotel, Andrea speaking. How may I help you?"

Angela was still shaking, "Good morning. John Simmons, please."

Andrea replied as if she were searching, "Ah... Oh there he is. Please hold."

The sounds of the hotel were replaced with soft background music. Angela held the phone to her ear for what seemed an eternity, and then the music stopped. It was replaced with a man's voice sounding deep, sweet, and curious, "Hello? John Simmons."

Angela couldn't believe it. It was finally him. She was terrified. This was Angela's truth, at last.

"Hello, Mr. Simmons. It's me, Angela. Angela Evans. er… Angela Michails."

There was a long silence. John wasn't sure what to say first. Angela could hear her own blood rushing through her veins. She didn't like the sound of it and wished the silence on the phone would end.

He finally spoke, "Angela. It's wonderful to finally hear your voice. I was wondering if you would call. That detective said you probably would."

Angela had been waiting for this moment for so long, she had rehearsed it so many times and had known exactly how it would unfold. She had planned every question, anticipated every response. She had thought about every aspect of the conversation and the eventual meeting. Now that it was finally here, she couldn't think of a thing to say.

John spoke again, "Angela? Are you there?" The silence had unnerved him also.

"Yes!" she almost screamed, and quickly got herself back under control, "Yes. I'm here. Sorry, I just don't know where to start." She could feel herself starting to cry and fought it.

John laughed, "I know the feeling. I hear you've been looking for me? For some time, I gather."

Controlled, she chuckled aloud, "Yeah, a while." She felt suddenly awkward. The phone was too impersonal for this. "Listen, I know it's pretty short notice, but would you like to meet me for dinner? Do you know Jack's?"

"Dinner?" he responded, a little unsure. "Yeah sure. Why not? Yes, I know it. When?"

"How about seven?" she was clearly thrilled.

"See you then," John replied and the phone went silent.

Angela hadn't noticed her mother standing behind her. "Was that him?"

Angela turned, "Yes, it was. How long have you been there?" asked Angela.

"Long enough," There was no emotion in Elaine's voice.

"Are you annoyed?" Angela couldn't read how her mother felt.

Elaine laughed, "No, dear, of course not. I told you last night, I trust you."

Angela was pleased, "Do you want to join us for dinner?"

Elaine thought seriously, and then replied, "I don't think so dear," her voice was thoughtful.

It had been Angela's quest. Elaine was curious about him, more curious than she had originally thought, but she wouldn't go tonight. If things went well, she could meet him another time. Angela walked over to her mother and put her arms around her. They stood in silence holding each other.

* * * * *

Angela's mind was so distracted with thoughts of the evening ahead she was unable to accomplish any work. By late afternoon, she finally gave up and went home to get ready.

She arrived at Jack's at quarter to seven. Walking through the front door, she saw John already sitting in the lobby. He was looking very sharp in a dark blue jacket and white shirt although she thought the bright red tie looked a little unnatural. A big smile lit up her face as she approached him.

John stood up as the young woman approached. He thought how beautiful she looked in her long white dress with her hair piled on top of her head. Her eyes sparkled like life itself. He was a little uneasy as he reached out his hand, "Angela?"

How sweet his voice sounded as she went past his hand to hug him. The embrace shocked him. She could feel him tense up and realized she had made her first mistake. Even though she had learned so much about him and felt she already knew him, she realized he knew virtually nothing about her. She was a stranger to him. She backed away sheepishly. "I apologize, Mr. Simmons." She reached out her right hand to him, "I'm Angela Evans. I am so very pleased to finally meet you."

He took her hand and feeling silly about his nervousness, he tried to smile it away. The waiter interrupted to escort them to their table. "Can I get you something from the bar," the waiter said as the two were seated.

John looked up at him, "Just a coffee, thank you".

Angela looked at John and then up at the waiter, "A cola for me, please."

Angela was still looking at John and feeling proud of the man sitting in front of her. She wanted to scream out to everyone in the restaurant, "This is my father."

He nervously looked around the restaurant and then at Angela, "So, do you come here often?"

She couldn't believe those were his first words, and she laughed out loud. He was visibly shaken by her laughter.

She stopped abruptly as she realized how nervous he was. "I'm sorry. How insensitive of me. Yes, this is my favorite place. We had our reception here."

He relaxed a little thinking, "Finally, a topic," then spoke aloud, "Yes. You're recently married, the detective mentioned that. Your husband, he's a good man?" He was genuinely interested.

She smiled, almost cooing, "Philip? He's the greatest. It's been over a month and I still feel like we are on our honeymoon."

"How does he feel about you coming here tonight to meet me?" John was decidedly cautious.

She thought for a second, "Well actually, he doesn't know. He's away on business".

Angela realized Philip was missing all of this. He had no idea that she had finally found her father. She had told him all about her quest many times, but he hadn't really shown much interest. She thought that he probably didn't think she would ever find him and didn't think he would care even if she did.

"On business? I see. What does he do?" asked John. He was glad to finally be engaged in conversation. They spent the next several hours talking and laughing, each bringing the other up to date on the events that formed their respective lives. She talked as if he was her father, and he talked trying to be what a father should be. A bond began to develop, not as pure as a true father and daughter, but as close as they two could come for now.

It was late and the restaurant was almost empty. The staff was busily cleaning up as Angela looked around and realized they should probably go. "Listen, dinner is on me."

John shook his head, "No. I can't let you..." he saw the look in Angela's eyes and he smiled, "Of course.

Thank you for a most pleasant evening. It has been fabulous meeting you. I certainly need more beautiful things in my life." He looked down at the empty cup in front of him. The waiter, who had been so attentive all evening, hadn't been seen in quite awhile.

Angela smiled at him, "Why don't we get together and continue this tomorrow?"

He looked at Angela sheepishly, "I have to work tomorrow."

She chuckled politely realizing that he couldn't drop everything to be with her, "Of course..." she paused, "how about dinner with me and my mother tomorrow night?"

He knew he definitely was not ready to meet the mother! It had been awkward enough meeting Angela. He felt almost guilty about her mother. He shook his head, "I don't know if I'm ready for that."

Angela understood immediately what he meant, "You're right. That might be awkward. What about my place tomorrow night? Just the two of us. I'd like to cook you dinner. Philip won't be back for a few more days."

He thought about that for a second, "Sure, why not?"

He had become very fond of Angela in the short time he had known her. He felt he was making a connection with the child he had always wanted. The specifics of it didn't matter to him at this point - she was his daughter. He knew for certain, he would do anything for her. "Dinner tomorrow, I'd like that." he said.

"Great, I'll see you then." He was content as Angela wrote her home address on the back of her business card.

After they had departed, she raced home to call her mother. She knew her mother would still be up and pictured her sitting in the living room, a fire blazing, sipping on her favorite wine and waiting for Angela's call. She would be so pleased for her. At least, Angela hoped she would be.

* * * * *

Angela was busily making all her last minute preparations for the evening. The table was set with the new china and crystal she had bought. Two tall white candles sat on the table already lit with a fresh floral centerpiece separating them. The aroma of the cooked food filled the air, and her favorite collection of Tchaikovsky was playing at an appropriate level. She looked around satisfied. The place looked perfect. All she needed was her father.

The door bell rang. When she opened the door John was standing there wearing the same suit as the night before. She thought it must be the only one he owned. He was looking down at the card in his hand and was startled when she opened the door.

Seeing Angela, he smiled, "I wasn't sure I was at the right place." Glancing around, he walked in, "Nice. Very nice indeed."

She could see he was surprised by the house, and pleased that he liked it. "It's a work in progress, I'm afraid."

He looked back at her, and smiled warmly, "Not at all. It looks great." He couldn't think of anything that could be missing as she led the way to the living room. Their footfalls echoed off the marble floors. Everything was in varying shades of white. A few carefully chosen pieces of art - paintings, sculpture and such were the only objects with real colour and these stood out in contrast, catching the eye. That had been her desire and design. A fire burned pleasantly in the fireplace. He thought how beautiful the whole place looked, like something out of a magazine, and he suddenly felt out of place.

Angela sensed his discomfort. "I've been trying to make this place feel a little bit homier. I've still got a ways to go."

He knew what she was trying to do and felt bad. "Well you've done a great job. You guys are obviously doing very well."

Blatant displays of wealth had always annoyed her. She had wanted him to see her home; she was not trying to intimidate. She was really bothered that he felt that way. This visit wasn't going the way she had hoped.

"Ah, why don't we go to Jack's, if you'll feel more comfortable." She was trying to make him feel better. It had the opposite effect.

"No. I'm okay. It's a bit of a surprise is all," he paused, "I'll be fine, really. Let's just have a nice evening." And he sat in the leather armchair. It was the only piece of Philip's original furniture that she had kept.

Angela poured coffee from the silver service, remembering how he took it - two lumps and a splash. Once it was prepared, she handed it to him.

Taking her own cup she sat on the couch and looked at him, "If you want, Mom can join us for dessert. I told her all about you. She'd like to meet you, if you'd like."

His head was still swimming. He nodded politely and thought, “One thing at a time,” then answered, "I'll let you know, okay?" and smiled softly. They sat for half an hour chatting. After dinner they returned to the living room, enjoying the afterglow of the meal they had just shared.

John started, "Call her."

Angela was caught off guard, "Sorry?"

"Your mother, give her a call. I think I would like to meet her."

Angela was thrilled. She quickly grabbed the phone.

Elaine arrived in fifteen minutes. She had been waiting, already dressed, just in case the call came. She wanted to meet him; it had become important to her.

Standing face to face in the living room, shaking hands, neither knew what to say.

Elaine started, "It's certainly a pleasure to meet you, John." This was the man that had made such an incredible difference in her life when his genes combined with hers, they had created the most incredible creature on Earth, Angela.

"Yes. I'm very pleased to meet you." John replied. She was older than he had expected. John continued, "Angela has certainly grown into a fine woman - a real testament to you, no doubt."

Elaine smiled pleasantly. This was every bit as awkward as Elaine had thought it would be. She felt an obligation to try and make him feel comfortable.

Looking at both of them, John felt something deep inside. Possibly it was guilt, or maybe it was joy, or compassion, or maybe terror. Perhaps it was all of that. Back then he had been so young. He had had no idea this day would ever come nor had he given any thought to the people it would affect. He had had no idea how significant his actions would be. He had had no thought of how whole worlds would be created - worlds that he was not a part of, and yet was significantly responsible for. For the first time, he wondered how many other worlds he had created. He became suddenly overwhelmed. He left as fast as he could without saying another word.

Angela was totally stunned and called after him, trying to make him stop. Why did he do that? What had she done? Where had her father gone? She felt hurt and confused.

Elaine stood looking at her daughter. A tear ran down her cheek. She had been afraid this would happen and had prayed it wouldn't. Elaine stayed with Angela late into the night.

* * * * *

Determined that it wasn't going to end this way, in the morning Angela phoned him. "Good Morning. Drake Hotel, Andrea speaking. How may I help you?"

Angela hesitated, then carried on, determined, "John Simmons, please."

Andrea sounded excited, "Is this Angela?"

Angela was surprised, "Yes, it is?"

Andrea was ecstatic, "John told us all about you. He was so excited." Then she paused and became serious, "Actually, John didn't come into work today. We're not sure where he is."

Angela was suddenly concerned for him. Andrea was quick to give Angela John's home address, believing he wouldn't mind. Angela hung up and headed for town.

When she reached John's building, Angela headed straight to his apartment. She found it easily and took a deep breath before knocking.

"Who is it?" was the response.

"It's me. Angela."

There was silence. She stood looking at the door for what seemed an eternity, finally it opened. John, in his bathrobe, looked at her for a second before inviting her in. John started speaking as she crossed the threshold. "Listen, I'm really sorry about last night. A lot of things were going through my head. I just had to get out of there. I had to think."

Angela looked at him and nodded her head knowingly. "Mom explained it to me. I didn't understand at first. I had to put myself in your shoes. I'm really sorry."

He smiled at her, "Have a seat."

She looked around the one room apartment. A neatly made single bed stood by the window. A galley kitchen area was off to one side and contained a small dining table and a couple chairs. A couch and an upholstered chair surrounded the coffee table. Most of the items in the room had seen better days. Prints of great art hung on the walls, somehow looked out of place. A bookshelf leaned against one wall, housing a small TV, a few books, magazines, and some personal items but the overall appearance was neat and tidy and simple. The whole place, she thought, wasn't the size of her own bedroom.

John noticed Angela looking around, "It's not much but its home."

She responded sincerely, "Not at all. It's very nice. It's you." She meant that in the most positive of ways and he took it as such.

Something caught her eye and she walked over to the bookshelf for a closer look. On one of the shelves was an unopened bottle of whisky against which leaned a very ornate, obviously antique, gilded picture frame.

John saw her interest, "That's a very personal piece. I call it 'Nemesis'," and he chuckled.

She looked back at him, and smiled. The tea kettle began singing its high pitched song. He fixed a pot and with a couple of cups joined Angela, "Its Earl Gray. I hope you like it."

She smiled and took a sip of tea before speaking, "I want to help you. I'll do anything I can." She reached into her purse and pulled out an envelope and handed it to him. "I have so much and you..." she stopped herself there.

He looked at her and saw the sincerity in her face and smiled taking the envelope. Inside was a large sum of cash; he was shocked at seeing it, "My god, Angela." He thought for a second and handed it back to her. "I can't accept this. I can't take your money. I don't have much but it's all I need. I'm doing fine."

She took the envelope back and put it on the coffee table in one motion. "You're doing incredibly well." she started, "I don't mean to imply..." She thought for a second, "I don't think I could survive what you have been through. Everybody needs money. Do something fun for yourself. Go on a trip. Go shopping. Take a woman out for dinner. Buy something you want."

He looked into her eyes and knew she wouldn't let it go, "Thank you, Angela. I'll do that."

He truly appreciated the gesture but didn't like the way it made him feel. He thought she probably solved many problems by throwing money at them. He believed all rich people did that and didn't think anything of it. Then he thought of her. She was his daughter and she was just trying to help out the old man. He wasn't really sure which was true, but decided it was the latter. He needed to believe that.

John sat up straight in his chair, "I'm going to start by taking you out for the day." He thought quickly,

"A walk in the park, lunch on the river." He hesitated again, "The afternoon at the amusement park and a nice dinner." He looked into her eyes and smiled, "A father and daughter day. Are you up to it?"

She smiled warmly at him, "Sounds great."

"Give me a couple of minutes to get dressed and we'll be off. I told the hotel I wasn't feeling well. It was true and this is just the medicine I need." He chuckled as he headed off to the bathroom. He knew it now. There was no doubt in his mind. He loved this girl.

12

Angela was excited that Philip was coming home, but she had to hurry as it was already four thirty and Philip's flight would be arriving in ninety minutes. She knew his trip had been successful, even before she talked to him. He would have done and said whatever it took to sell the prospect, and when he returned home, he would make those promises a reality. The whole process came so naturally to him - it was a gift.

However, it was Angela's past few days that were uppermost in her mind. To her, these days had been far more important than Philip's latest business success. She knew Philip would be eager to hear all about the new developments and that he would be happy for her. As she hurried to the front door of her home, Angela could hear Philip's favourite music coming from inside. Eagerly, she opened the door.

Philip was sitting in his leather armchair facing the unlit fireplace. His eyes were closed and he held a glass of sherry in his hand; he was obviously engrossed in the music. She rushed over and jumped into his lap like a tiger pouncing on its prey. The glass fell from his hand, smashing on the floor. Angela giggled at Philip's shocked look.

She spoke excitedly, "You're early!" and she locked him into a long, passionate kiss.

When she paused, he laughed, "My God, I'm going to have to go away more often, just so I can home again."

She giggled, "I have so much to tell you! How was your trip?"

He shrugged his shoulders and was about to say something but Angela continued before he had a chance.

"I missed you so much. I've had the most incredible couple of days. So much has happened. You're going to be so happy."

Angela started to recount everything she and her father had done, and how her feelings for him had grown. She looked and sounded like a giddy school girl, full of pure and innocent joy.

Philip had been sitting in his chair contemplating his trip. He had come home early to unwind and Angela's exuberance and high energy dazed him.

He vaguely recalled her telling him something about the quest she had been on. He now wished he had paid more attention originally. It was almost as if he was hearing it for the first time.

As her story unfolded, he became more and more uneasy. His concerns and suspicions may be legitimate, or they could simply be confusion and needed time to sort it all out so he decided to leave his comments until tomorrow. He didn't want to interfere with her joy. Tonight he was going to take every advantage of her jubilance. They skipped dinner and retired early.

* * * * *

When Philip woke his mind recalled the previous night. He couldn't remember Angela ever being so creative. He was so incredibly satisfied and fulfilled. She had made him feel like a king - a master of the universe. He thought how love made sex better. He was experiencing an all consuming belief that his very soul had been enlarged - his very being had been altered.

Angela was moving around the kitchen preparing breakfast when Philip entered. Her smile made her whole face glow and Philip thought how remarkable she looked.

She was so happy about her father and Philip's obvious support of her. She had planned to take the tray to him in bed, but now placed it on the table.

He watched her move and thought about the stories she had shared last night. He began to think his suspicions were unfounded. How could this incredible creature be wrong? It wasn't possible.

"You didn't tell me," Angela started, "Did you bag another one." She was talking about the business meetings, but his first thought was something else. "Pardon!?" his voice cracked.

She looked at him, "Your meetings, whoever he was, did you land the deal with him?"

He laughed out loud. "Yes! Henry! Great guy! We're a lot alike, he and I. We had a lot of fun. I think he'll be a good one."

Angela smiled having missed his momentary trauma. Philip was tortured as he recalled his begging and the sinister look on Lisa's face as she assured him of her silence. She now possessed information that was of great value, and he knew she would eventually use it. He silently hoped it would only be money that Lisa would demand.

"It was the last time," he had told himself and he had meant it - even before he knew it was Lisa. Such things were no longer important to him, but now he was terrified Angela might find out. He finally realized that Angela was all he wanted, and he was truly afraid.

Angela joined him with the food. He was very hungry, but his memories seasoned the otherwise pleasant morning feast with guilt. He hoped Angela wouldn't continue talking about his trip. A defensive offense was his only hope, and he quickly changed the subject.

"Listen, Angela. I have some concerns about this Simmons character." He hesitated, trying to be gentle. "What do you really know about this guy?"

Angela was immediately defensive, "What do you mean? I know everything about him. I told you last night."

Philip took another bite of his breakfast, trying to make the conversation appear casual. "It just seems odd to me. This guy appears virtually out of nowhere, takes your money, wines and dines you..."

Angela's emotions were blossoming into anger, "You know damn well what I've gone through to find him."

He nodded and continued eating. "I do know, Ange." Then he thought, "Well not really."

He continued, "It's just that this whole thing makes me nervous. It just seems like he's running a game on you. What's his motivation? You're nothing to him - a lab experiment or something." He immediately wished he hadn't said that.

Angela was visibly stunned, "Motivation? Experiment? Are you insane? The man has been to hell and back. I'm the only thing he has."

Now Philip was getting angry. He wasn't sure if his anger was at her for not understanding what he was saying or himself for bringing up the topic in the first place.

He looked at her directly. "The man had a life. He had his own world. He was doing just fine. You come along and he drops everything. Suddenly, he's all over you. He's with you everyday. Obviously he's trying to build trust and rapport. I just can't help thinking he's setting you up for something."

Angela suddenly became calm which made Philip uneasy. Her voice marginally louder than a whisper, "I was going to ask you to give him a job. I was hoping to make him a direct part of our life. I wanted so much for you to meet him. I was sure you would be happy for me. Now I'm not sure I even know you."

"Come on, Angela. Don't you think you're over-reacting? I am happy for you, really. I just think we need to find out a little more about this guy before we get involved."

"Over-reacting," her temper flared. "Can't you see how happy he's made me? How much he means to me? My God, Philip, he's my father - the man that gave me life. You wouldn't have me as your wife, if it wasn't for him."

"How can you be so sure?" Philip boiled. "You said yourself, the trail was cold. The detective had a hell of a time finding this guy. Maybe he found the wrong one. Maybe that PI is in on the whole scam. Have you thought about a DNA test before you hand everything over to him?" He instantly knew that was a mistake too.

Angela looked at Philip, stunned. She couldn't believe the things he was saying. "This is madness," she thought, "What is wrong with you?"

Philip thought, "This is getting way out of control." A wedge was being driven between them. He continued sternly "I don't want you to see him anymore, do you understand? It stops right now. I don't know what this guy's game is, but it stops now. I want some time to check him out."

Angela was furious. She looked at him hard, then got up and ran out of the house. When the front door slammed shut, he hammered his fist on the top of the table, "Damn!" He could put together million dollar deals, but he couldn't get his wife to understand reason. He got up from the table and went for the phone.

"Hello, Jock. Philip Evans. I have a job for you."

"Sure thing, Mr. Evans. What's up?"

Jock was an investigator Philip had used on many occasions for his business and wanted him to investigate John. Jock would find the truth and Philip needed to know if his suspicions were accurate, for himself as much as for Angela.

* * * * *

Angela drove aimlessly for hours thinking and trying to decide what she was going to do. She eventually found herself at her mother's door. Elaine wasn't home, but Angela went in anyway. She poured herself a glass of wine and went upstairs to her old room. A bubble bath always relaxed her, and if nothing else, it would give her a chance to think.

When Elaine arrived home she found Angela asleep on the couch. She didn't know why Angela was there, but it didn't matter, she was happy to see her daughter. Brushing Angela's hair from her face, she gave her daughter a gentle kiss. Angela woke and for an instant, everything was right in the world. All too quickly the memories rushed back and she began to cry.

"What's wrong, dear?" Elaine spoke softly but was concerned.

"We had a terrible fight. He can be such a jerk. I hate him," Angela started, then proceeded to tell her mother the whole tale.

Elaine didn't speak until she was certain Angela had finished, "So what are you going to do now?"

Elaine understood Philip's concerns; she had had the same feelings in the beginning. It was only after she had met John that her opinion changed.

"I don't know what I'm going to do. I just know that I can't go back there." Angela was still sobbing.

Elaine held Angela and said, "I think you should go home and talk to Philip."

"I can't, Mom. He just doesn't understand." Angela responded

Elaine thought it better not to push. "All right then, stay here tonight, but please don't let this go on too long. You have to talk to him. He's not a stupid man, he just doesn't understand. Give him a chance. Explain it to him. Make him understand, but stay calm. Yelling and screaming doesn't solve anything."

Angela knew her mother was right; she had reached the same conclusion. She loved Philip, but had been completely horrified by his comments.

"Angela you must learn to deal with your marital problems. You have to work things out with him." Elaine finished. She was going to stay out of this, but it wasn't going to be easy, after all this was her daughter.

* * * * *

Philip had met Mike for drinks in the afternoon and arrived home later than usual. He knew Mike wouldn't be able to offer any viable solutions, but he had hoped that by talking to him he might be able to see things more clearly himself.

As Philip entered the house, a new sensation came over him. He could see Angela's touch everywhere. Her spirit filled every corner, but she wasn't there and Philip felt the worst kind of emptiness.

Reaching for the phone, Philip hoped Angela was at her mother's house. He needed his wife home, no matter the cost. He started to dial and then stopped and hung it up. He would give her a chance to calm down and think. Perhaps Elaine would be able to get through to her. Tomorrow they would talk; maybe even have her father over for dinner. Tomorrow everything would be fine.

* * * * *

Angela and her mother had prepared a simple supper in silence. Each had been engaged in their own thoughts, thinking of things they would be discussing later.

Afterwards, they sat together in the living room and began talking. They discussed the realities of relationships. The willow and the wind - bend and grow, her mother had said.

Men just think differently, her mother had also said. All those little things that women love in them are the very things that cause the problems. "Philip's heart is in the right place, Angela. He believes he is acting in your best interest. He feels he is protecting you." Elaine said.

By midnight the topics were as completely exhausted as they were and Angela was feeling much better. It all made sense to her now. Angela knew her mother was right, but she knew Philip was right also. Tomorrow they would be able to work it all out. Tomorrow everything would be fine.

13

The annoying sound of the telephone woke her. Only slightly conscious, Angela glanced at the night table clock and smiled – 10:06 a.m. "That must be Philip calling to beg forgiveness," she thought as she picked up the receiver. "Hello?"

"Ange? Janet."

"Janet? Good morning. You're up early." Angela wasn't used to hearing from Janet before noon. Angela wiped the sleep from her eyes as she waited for Janet to begin.

"Angela, are you still in bed?" Janet sounded surprised.

"No. I had to get up to answer the phone." Angela chuckled.

Janet continued, "What the hell are you doing at your Mom's? I tried your place but there was no answer."

At first, Angela thought Philip must have gone to the office but then thought, "It's Sunday. Why would he go to the office?" She became angry again; Philip was supposed to be at home pining for her, it was the least he could do. "Philip and I had a big fight about my father yesterday. I just..."

Janet interrupted, "Listen, Ange. We have to talk. Something's come up you need to know." Janet's voice sounded far too serious.

Angela was concerned, "My God, Janet, what is it? You okay?"

"I'm fine. Not on the phone, girlfriend. I'm coming over. I'll be there in thirty minutes, so get out of bed," and Janet hung up.

"Something must be very wrong," Angela thought. She got up, dressed, and went to the kitchen to put on coffee. Reaching for the coffee carafe she spotted the note her mother had left.

"Good morning, Dear.
I have a few things I need to take care of at the office. I'll be home in a couple of hours. There are some bagels on the counter and cream cheese in the refrigerator. See you soon, Love Mom"

Angela smiled, thinking how dedicated her mother was to the business - even on a Sunday.

When the coffee was ready she poured herself a cup and put the rest in a thermal carafe. Before long the doorbell rang and Janet walked in. The ringing of the doorbell was merely formality; Janet had no intention of waiting for a response. She was breathing hard and the look on her face made Angela's heart skip, "My God, Janet. What's going on?"

Janet put both her hands out in front of her, and tried to catch her breath. "Ange, sit down." Angela wasn't standing and she half screamed at her friend, "Janet!?"

Janet looked down at Angela, shook her head and sat beside her. Angela's patience waned, "Janet!?"

Janet gathered her thoughts, "Okay. Okay." she paused, the direct method was best she thought. "Philip is screwing around on you."

Angela was almost relieved. She calmed down when she realized that was all of it. The events of five months ago rushed forward from the depths of her memory. She was sure she had discussed the whole matter with Janet back then.

"Janet! I thought it was something serious. That's old news." She paused, "I told you about all that back then. Philip and I had that huge fight and I almost called off the wedding. Don't you remember?" Angela had been so enraged at Philip. He thought that since they weren't married he wasn't doing anything wrong. He vowed that he would never be with anyone else ever again. Her trust in him returned slowly and she decided not to let it stand in their way.

Janet was shaking her head. "No, No. Not that. I remember that. Believe me, I remember." Angela's tears had ruined Janet's favorite silk blouse - she wore cotton today.

"He's never stopped. He's screwed around on you on almost every trip since then - including the last one!" Janet's voice cracked as she spoke but she knew she had an obligation to tell Angela no matter how much it was going to hurt her.

Angela sat on the couch in disbelief; feeling like something deep inside her was being ripped out by the roots. She started shaking, and her voice was almost a whisper, "What?" Janet looked at her compassionately and nodded confirmation.

Janet continued, "Mike told me last night while we... Well, after we... Mike told me last night. He made me promise not to tell you." Janet was getting angry, "He talked as if Philip was his hero or something. Philip had said it had been the last time. Mike was proud of him for that or something. Who knows what goes on in men's heads, I just couldn't believe it."

Janet had no doubt of the story's validity. She often said, "The only time men tell the truth is in a death bed confession or as pillow talk after they have been satisfied." She wouldn't have said anything to Angela if she weren't absolutely sure and Angela knew it.

Angela began to cry and Janet reached out and took her in her arms, "I'm really sorry, Ange. Men can be such pigs. It's really the reason I try to avoid getting too serious with them." That revelation didn't help. Angela buried her face in her girlfriends shoulder and wept uncontrollably.

Just as suddenly, Angela stopped crying and straightened up, startling Janet. Her expression was cold and it made Janet shiver. Rage was building inside Angela and when she spoke her voice sounded alien, "That bastard! He's going to pay for this." Angela got up, pushing Janet aside as she strode from the house. Janet ran after her pleading for her to stop. Angela ignored her as she continued to her car. Janet gave up the pursuit at the front door and stood watching as Angela drove away. She felt so totally helpless, wanting desperately to do something but realizing that there was nothing anyone could do. When Angela was out of sight, she went back inside and began to cry.

The phone rang and instinctively Janet answered it.

"Janet?" Philip was surprised to hear her voice. "Is Angela there?"

"No, you pig. She's gone out." Janet didn't attempt to hide her feelings. Philip was instantly angry and confused, "Pig? What's going on, Jan?"

"She knows, you bastard. I told her. She knows everything." With that, she hung up the phone.

Philip sat in his office still holding the phone to his ear, stunned. Replacing it, he realized what had happened. He muttered under his breath, "Mike". At that moment he wanted to kill Mike.

Philip knew he would never be unfaithful again, but that didn't matter now. Angela had found out and she would never trust him again. He didn't know what he was going to do or what Angela would do. He felt his whole world was about to come crashing down. He was more desperate now about the future than he had ever been in his life.

He remembered all the things he had done in the past and how sorry he was now. However, it had happened, and was a part of history forever. There was nothing he could do about the past; all he could do was try to fix the now - and the future.

He had no idea where Angela was or how much damage had been done. He wished he had called her before he had left the house. He had to deal with this appointment first and then he would go find her. He had to try to make it right - he had to.

* * * * *

Angela was heading to her mother's office but arrived at the Drake Hotel instead. She found John easily and he immediately saw she was in trouble, "Angela, what's the matter?"

Angela had stopped crying, "Can you talk?"

"Of course, of course," and he put his arm around her shoulder. As they passed the front desk John glanced at Andrea and pointed to his watch. Seeing that Angela needed him, Andrea nodded her approval of his early break.

John led Angela into the staff lounge and sat her on the only couch. He hurried to the sink to get her a glass of water, and then joined her on the couch.

"Okay, Angela. Tell me what's wrong." There was a certain pride in the realization that she needed him. He had no idea what was wrong, but knew he would do whatever he could to help her.

Angela had trouble getting started. She thought if she didn't actually say the words then maybe it never happened but she knew it had and she needed to talk about it.

She began telling John about Philip's early affairs, and continued through to the information Janet had relayed this morning. John grew angrier as her story progressed. He was forming an opinion about the kind of person Philip was and he didn't like him.

He searched his mind for just the right words to say but none came. He couldn't decide if she expected him to actually say anything or if she just wanted him to listen. He hoped it was the latter. All he could say was, "I'm so sorry, Angela. I'm so sorry." Saying those words made him feel even more helpless.

When she had finished, Angela got up and went to the sink for another glass of water. She knew the next thing she would tell was going to be equally as difficult. With her back to John, she told him everything Philip had said about him and how he didn't want her to see him anymore. Her voice cracked at almost ever syllable.

John had been upset about Philip's affairs, but this news enraged him. "How could someone be so cruel? How could Angela be married to such a beast? She deserved so much more." He thought.

Only after she finished could she turn and face the hurt and anger she knew would be there. "I just don't know what to do. He's my husband. I only hope that I can convince him that he's wrong about you."

John was devastated and the first thing that came to his mind was, "What does your mother think about all this?" Hearing his words, he wished he had said something else.

"Well. She did say that she had had some of the same concerns."

John's face dropped. His only interest had been in making a connection with Angela. Now he didn't know what was right or wrong.

Angela saw his anguish, "She has changed her mind since she met you. She said your eyes told her the truth. She knew you were who I had hoped you would be. She was sure of it. She said she could see you in me."

Just as quickly he felt better. He never understood how women could tell lineage with a glance. They hadn't been together very long that night before he had stormed out. Remembering that, he said, "About the other night, I'm really sorry I took off like I did. I just got very scared with your mother there and all. I thought I could handle it but I was wrong. I'm sorry."

She smiled at him. It felt good to smile again. "Not at all. Mom understood. She really did. Besides, we've already talked about that, remember."

John remembered the conversation, but felt an obligation to apologize anyway. He walked over to Angela and put his hands on her shoulders and looked into her eyes. "Listen Angela, I love you. I know that now. Like nothing I have ever loved before. I really need you to believe that. But I really don't know what we are going to do." He paused, "I think you should go now. Go back to your mother's or something. I need a little time to try and figure things out. Don't talk to Philip for a few days. Let the bastard wallow in his guilt for awhile. He has said and done some pretty awful things. I have to think. You need some time, too."

John realized that he had been preoccupied with Philip's assault of him. He had put Philip's infidelities on some back burner, like they were of much less importance. He knew that was not true. They were actually the most important thing. He felt bad about his selfishness, and that made him dislike Philip even more.

Angela was surprised by John's sudden change of emotion. She had come to be consoled but now she was feeling concern for him. She didn't want to leave him like this but could see how badly he wanted her to go. As she was heading for the door he called to her, his voice totally void of emotion. "Angela, do you still love him?"

Angela stopped in her tracks, shocked by the question, stunned by his tone. She had only been thinking about the things Philip had done. She hesitated, and then turned to face John. The look in her eyes answered his question, "That's all I need to know. I will call you tomorrow. Tonight you rest. Don't worry sweetheart. No one is going to get between us. I'll come up with something."

* * * * *

John sat in his apartment in silence. He hadn't been able to concentrate at work after Angela left. Andrea had offered her assistance but that wasn't what he needed. She promised to cover for him and he left for the day.

Sitting there, he looked over at "Nemesis". The object almost screamed with all the pain and suffering it represented. He wept. All he had ever wanted was a good woman by his side and a few kids – a family. He wondered if that had really been so much to ask. He knew Angela was the only thing in the world that would prove he had existed at all and he wondered what he had done that condemned him to live this life.

John looked around his apartment and for the first time thought how pitiful it looked. He remembered the elegance of Angela's house and how everything in her world was so beautiful. Then he thought how Philip was trying to take his daughter away from him.

John laughed at himself, "My daughter? Who am I kidding? The bastard's right. She's not much more that a lab experiment." He didn't really believe that. She was undeniably a part of him. "I had no idea what I was doing. I wasn't in it to create life - I was in it for the bucks, but now this beautiful creature..." His mind was on fire and his emotions were being torn in every direction. He was losing the ability to discern right from wrong. He looked at "Nemesis" again. He couldn't think straight. The cap came off.

14

As Angela rounded the bend to her mother's house, she could see Philip's Ferrari in the driveway. Just for a moment she considered driving by. Instead, she pulled up the drive and passed his car. Acting as if she hadn't seen him, she casually strolled towards the front door. She felt his hand on her arm and his voice sounded pitiful, "Angela, please. We have to talk." Rage started building in her and she spun to look at him. She could see his pain but she didn't care. She realized the answer to her father's question was, "NO!" She knew without doubt that her love for Philip was gone.

The sparkle in Angela's eyes that had existed just for him was gone. Those eyes now looked upon him with the coldness of death. He released her arm and felt suddenly empty, "I've lost you, haven't I?"

The blood roared almost audibly through Angela's veins - pure hate had encompassed her totally. "Get... out... of... my... face..., you bastard!" was all she could say. Her voice sounded like the devil incarnate.

He hadn't openly cried since a child but tears were in his eyes now, "Please, Angela. I love you. Talk to..."

The items Angela had been carrying hit the ground as her hand curled and struck the side of the face. Her fist was tight and the wedding set she wore opened his cheek as effectively as a surgeon's scalpel - but without the precision. He reeled from the impact. She was only marginally aware that it had been her hand that had caused this reaction - it was surreal.

On the ground, Philip pulled his hand from the wound and gazed in disbelief at his own blood. His eyes returned to Angela, and he couldn't see any emotion at all on her face. He knew there was no point, it was over. He got up off the ground and left. Angela watched him drive away and then continued into the house as if nothing had happened. No tears; no pain; no pleasure; no regrets - she felt absolutely nothing. The light in her soul had been extinguished.

Inside she noticed the light flashing on the answering machine and pushed the replay button. "Hi Angela, it's Mom" Angela chuckled at that. Of course she knew her mother's voice. "I'm working late. Something has come up. I hope you patched things up with Philip and you don't get this message." Angela thought, "How sweet - so typically Mom." Angela felt her mother would be proud of her behaviour today, but thinking more, Angela realized she probably wouldn't be. The machine beeped, and the next message began.

"Angela, John Simmons... um, sorry, your father here." he sounded like he had been drinking. "I've been giving this a lot of thought. I can't have this in my life right now. It's too hard. I've caused you so much grief. We've met and I will always be grateful for having known you. I'm going away. I still have some of the money you gave me. It's enough to get me started somewhere. Now that I know you, I will contact you in awhile, again, maybe. I don't know. I've caused you so much grief. I have to go..." and the machine went silent.

Angela stood looking at that heartless device. She couldn't believe what she had heard. He can't go, he can't. She started beating on the machine with both hands, it rewound and erased, and she kept hitting it. The "on" light finally gave up and the machine lay silently in pieces. She stood looking at its now pitiful state and felt bad. She had to stop him. She had worked too hard to find him and she rushed out of the house.

Angela stood banging on John's door, yelling his name. A neighbor, hearing the ruckus, came into the hall. He was annoyed by the noise, "He's not there, damn it."

Angela spun and looked at him. He saw the total desperation on her face. She sobbed, "Do you know where he went?"

The man calmed down at seeing her and shook his head. "Sorry Miss. He didn't say. He had a couple suitcases in his hand. I don't think he's coming back."

Angela's heart sank, "Thank you."

She looked back at the door she had been beating. She gently brushed her hand against it as if she was apologizing - or perhaps just saying good-bye. She walked out into the street and looked up and down in each direction hoping to catch a glimpse of him walking away.

The sign of the Drake Hotel caught Angela's eye. It was closer than she remembered and she walked towards it. Her sadness was obvious but there were no tears left. She had cried everything she had.

In the lobby, a young woman was standing at the desk. Angela read the name "Andrea" on her name tag. Although she had been there the other day, but she hadn't really seen her.

Andrea watched Angela's approach, and was shaking her head before Angela could say anything. Angela had to ask anyway. Andrea just replied solemnly, "He didn't say where he was going. He picked up his last cheque and left. We are sure going to miss him around here. He had such a passion for life. He was so pleased at having met you. You were all he talked about. I'm really sorry. I don't know what happened."

Angela smiled thoughtfully, and turned back to the street. She had no intention of telling Andrea what had happened. It wasn't any of her business. Walking back to her car Angela thought of Janet. She needed her now. Janet always had a way of making Angela feel better. Whatever the problem, Janet's simplistic ways put everything into perspective.

When Angela arrived at Janet's apartment door, she could hear Janet and Mike yelling at each other. She couldn't hear what they were saying but was sure she knew what the fight was about. They hadn't done anything to deserve this and she felt she had no right bringing them in any deeper, so she left.

The beach was also a calming place for Angela's soul. She walked for hours, trying to sort things out in her mind. So much had happened lately. "How did things go so wrong? This just can't be my life!" she thought. The color of sky changed from blue to the most spectacular shades of red, and purple and pink and lavender and yellow. She was glad she had been here to witness it, but all too soon it was gone and the blackness of night engulfed her. The moon was high in the sky before she started back to her mother's. Angela was ready to talk now.

The house was dark - Elaine had obviously gone to bed. If her mother had known the events of the day, Angela knew she would have been waiting for her. Angela remembered the answering machine with regret - that wouldn't be giving any answers either. She considered waking her mother, but decided to let her sleep. The morning would come and she would talk to her mother then. Tomorrow; there's always tomorrow. That notion didn't provide solace.

15

Sam heard the telephone ringing and tried to fit the sound into the dream he was enjoying. He woke slowly and the ringing grew louder as he proceeded through the stages of sleep toward consciousness. Glancing at the bedside clock he cursed under his breath. Four twenty it read as he picked up the telephone receiver. He thought quickly of just slamming it back down, but brought it to his ear instead. His voice was almost alert, "Davidson here! What do you want?"

The voice on the other end was all too familiar. Sam had been awakened from many a pleasant slumber by this same voice. It wasn't a pleasant sound, but it did have the effect of waking him completely. The dispatcher gave Sam all the details he needed. All were now written on the notepad beside the phone.

Sam reviewed the note quickly before he spoke, "Listen, call Williams and have him meet me at the beach. But do me a favor; give me forty minutes before you call. Thanks."

The dispatcher hesitated, and then agreed, unsure of the delay or why he should be making the call to Sam's partner at all. However, receiving unusual requests from Sam during these early morning calls was normal and he just added this one to the growing list he mentally maintained.

Hanging up, Sam looked to the other side of his bed. It was empty and he sighed, "Damn, just a dream." He got up, dressed, and grabbed the notepad as he headed for the door.

Five fifteen, Williams arrived at the scene. Sam noticed his arrival and chuckled to himself, "He made pretty good time."

Sam was interviewing the young couple that had discovered the body as Williams approached. Williams was angry as he spoke, "Why the hell didn't you call me? How long have you been here?"

Sam looked up from his notepad and smiled, "Ah, good morning. Nice of you to join us" With his pen in hand he pointed to the car "Looks like a suicide."

Williams' eyes followed the line of the pen and saw the red Ferrari. The driver's door was open and the body inside was clearly visible. Williams hadn't noticed it when he had first arrived. He looked back toward Sam as he was dismissing the couple and realized he had missed the interview as well.

Sam walked toward his partner and gave him a friendly slap on the shoulder, "Ah, no worries. I've slept in on a few over the years myself."

Williams looked at him, puzzled. He thought for a second and decided that it wasn't Sam's fault at all, "Yeah sorry, dispatch screwed up, I guess."

Sam smiled knowingly and looked toward the car. Williams started walking towards it. "So, suicide is it?" As Williams approached, he made mental notes of how the car was parked and which direction it was pointed, the fact the door was open, and the position of the body. Once beside the driver's door he squatted and surveyed the interior of the car. The man inside was well dressed. The suit he wore was obviously very expensive.

The Ferrari was a few years old, but looked to be immaculately maintained. Williams liked Ferrari - always had. He recognized this model immediately as a 328i. It was painted in classic Ferrari red and appointed with the fine tan leather interior. It was exactly the car he would own - if he had the money and a different life.

Williams spoke with a sarcastic tone, "Well I can certainly understand why he would be depressed enough to kill himself. He is obviously rich and has one hell of a nice car. I'm sure I'd want to blow my brains out, too." Then his attention went back to the body in the driver's seat. The entry wound was directly above the bridge of the man's nose. The interior of the car was covered with the classic exit debris - blood, bone fragments, and cranial matter. He shook his head at the sight of it. The waste blended with the aroma of the oiled leather to create a scent that once experienced, is never forgotten – sweet; pungent; primal.

Williams thought to himself, "Where's the gun - and the note. What the hell's going on?" He stood up and faced his partner. He was about to inquire about those two vital pieces of evidence, but realized it had already been the better part of an hour. He was sure Sam had already sent them to the lab. He decided not to pursue it and accepted his partner's conclusion - suicide.

Sam watched Williams' changing expressions and thought he knew what was coming, but when his partner didn't say anything, Sam was genuinely surprised. He had prepared an entire speech to account for the missing items and was disappointed when Williams didn't query him. Then Sam thought, "Disappointed isn't the right word," it was more like disgust. Williams should have questioned him about those things. Maybe the Lieutenant was right.

Williams continued, "Do we have a name?"

Sam flipped back a few pages in his notepad, "Ah yeah. … Here it is…Evans. Philip Evans."

16

Once again it was very late before Angela was able to drift off to sleep. Only a few hours had passed before she was awakened by the sound of the door bell. She focused on the clock and mumbled, "Seven o'clock, who could that be?"

Forcing herself out of bed and donning her robe, she proceeded downstairs. Elaine had already answered the door. She could hear her mother talking to two men. The younger of the two noticed Angela first. The man's distraction caught Elaine's attention and she turned.

"Oh, Angela? You are here? These officers would like to talk to you."

Elaine escorted them to the living room where Angela joined them. The older of the two spoke first as he handed Angela his business card, "Mrs. Evans, I'm Detective Davidson." Then he gestured the other man, "This is my partner, Detective Williams."

Angela took the card, "What's going on?"

Sam continued, "Mrs. Evans, we're sorry to inform you that your husband, Philip Evans, was found dead early this morning."

Angela stood silently for a second, then her face lost all colour, and she collapsed towards the floor. Elaine shrieked and tried to catch Angela, but Sam was already there. Together they managed Angela to the couch. It took a few seconds for Angela to refocus.

The detective's words echoed in her mind. She looked at Sam, "My God, what happened?"

Sam continued in a matter-of-fact tone, "He was found at three this morning by a young couple near the beach. He had apparently committed suicide."

Angela shook her head, "Philip! My God, Philip!" The words were replayed over and over in her mind. "Philip? Suicide? No way! Not him!"

Sam carefully observed Angela's reactions - noting every subtle change in tone, body movement, and expression. Hardened by years on the job, it took Sam considerable effort to show compassion, "I'm sorry, Ma'am, but we did find a revolver in his hand and a typed letter in the car. It was certainly made to look like suicide."

Angela and Elaine caught it at the same time. Angela sounded stupefied, "Look like a suicide? What are you saying? He was murdered?"

Sam continued, "What happened to your hand, Mrs. Evans?"

She glanced quickly at her wedding ring and bruised knuckles. Philip's blood dulled the luster of diamonds and there were discernible pieces of flesh stuck in the clasps. She hadn't noticed that last night. If she had, she would have washed it off. She touched her hand and remembered the last time she saw Philip. All she could say was, "We had a fight and I hit him."

Williams spoke sarcastically, "Well, I guess we know where that cut came from."

Sam nodded his head, but was annoyed by his partner's tone. He tried to ignore it and continued with his questions, "Mrs. Evans can you tell us where you were between 11:00 p.m. and 3:00 a.m. last night?"

Elaine immediately understood where Sam's questions were leading. She became quite indignant, and protective of her daughter, "Quiet, Angela. Don't say another word." Angela was shocked by her mother's tone. "Wha..."

Elaine looked down, putting her hand on Angela's shoulder, "Trust me, don't say another word until I call Simon."

Angela looked at her hand again and realized what her mother meant. Then she looked back at the detectives, "You think I killed Philip? My God, he was my husband. I love him."

She suddenly thought about her father and what he had said. She thought that maybe he had something to do with this, but quickly thought, "No way, he wouldn't."

Sam stared at Elaine but spoke to Angela, "Mrs. Evans, I'm not accusing you of anything. Our investigation has only just started. We are interviewing everyone that may have seen him last night. We are simply trying to get a picture of what happened. We may very well find that it was suicide. We just want to know everything you did last night, that's all." Williams smiled, but it wasn't a comforting smile.

Angela decided to listen to her mother, "Look, I understand what you are doing. I know I didn't do this. My God, he was my husband. If you have any more questions for me, I think I should have my attorney present." She spoke as if someone were putting the words in her mouth. She looked at her mother and smiled.

Sam nodded his head and made no attempt to mask his disappointment. Elaine was standing with her hand on her daughter's shoulder and Sam knew the interview was over. "Mrs. Evans. Please don't plan any trips. We will want to talk to you again, soon. I promise you." He looked at Williams and gestured towards the door. Williams was shocked as he reluctantly followed Sam.

Outside Williams stopped and looked at his partner. "What the hell was that all about? This is bull shit. We should take her in for questioning at least. She wants to talk to her lawyer, fine. Let him come down there. She's hiding something, I can feel it. I say we take her in, now!"

Sam didn't miss a step as he walked toward the car - his voice was sure, "She had nothing to do with it."

Williams boiled, "What the hell? You saw her hand. You know the stats. She's the spouse. I'll bet a month's wages that she's the one that popped him in the head."

Sam laughed, and shook his own head. "I'll take that bet." He was glad that Williams had finally indicated his belief that it was murder. Clearly he hadn't believed the suicide explanation Sam had given at the scene. Maybe there was hope for him after all.

Closing the door behind the two policemen, Elaine almost collapsed herself. Letting out a deep breath she joined her daughter on the couch. Elaine looked into her daughter's eyes, her voice was insecure, "Angela, tell me everything. What happened yesterday? Something must have happened. Philip just isn't the kind of man that would kill himself."

Angela thought maybe she should have told the police everything then and there. Now it would look like she had been trying to hide something. It was the first time she ever questioned her mother's judgment but just as quickly she realized her mother was advising her without all the facts.

Angela recounted every step she had taken that day including her late night walk on the beach. Elaine listened quietly and knew how the day's activities would appear. She became increasingly worried for her daughter and hoped Simon would be able to help.

Elaine reached for the phone and dialed it from memory. She felt sudden relief at hearing Simon's voice. She skipped the pleasantries and started to explain what had happened. Her voice was cracking as she spoke, and the story sounded disjointed.

"Simon, you've got to help us. The police were here. They think she killed him. You have to help her. Yo....."

Simon stopped her, "Elaine you're not making any sense. You need to calm down."

Elaine became annoyed as she realized she was babbling. She didn't like to appear out of control but she also knew that if anyone understood, it would be Simon. "Philip's dead. They think Angela did it."

Simon realized what she was talking about, "Are they still there?"

"No, they left, but they made it clear that they would be back."

Simon smiled, "Well that's a very good sign. If they really thought Angela had something to do with it, you would be calling me from the station, believe me. You and Angela had better meet me at my office in an hour. I want to hear about everything. Okay?"

Elaine felt better. "Of course, Simon, we'll see you in an hour." She hung up and looked at her daughter. "I don't think we have anything to worry about sweetheart. Go get dressed. We're going to see Simon."

She had only heard her mother's side of the conversation, but the sudden change in her demeanor made Angela feel more comfortable and she headed up the stairs to her room.

17

The office had not yet opened for the day as Angela and Elaine entered the empty reception area and continued through to Simon's office. He was sitting behind his desk, deep in conversation with another man. Although they recognized the other man, they didn't really know him. Smaller in stature than Simon, he appeared to be in good shape. He wore a dark suit and his light brown hair and thick mustache were neatly trimmed.

Simon stopped talking and stood up as Angela and Elaine entered. He was wearing his usual dark suit and white shirt. Simon came around his desk and walked to Elaine. He smiled as he gave her a warm kiss and a genuine embrace. They had been seeing each other regularly since the wedding.

Angela, who hadn't been aware of the developing relationship, smiled. She was glad to see her mother interested in someone, and pleased that Simon was that someone.

Simon stepped away from Elaine and reached for Angela. He gave her a friendly hug and kissed her forehead before returning to his desk. The newspaper on his desk caught Angela's eye and she picked it up. On the front page was a large picture of Philip. The headline read, "Local millionaire and philanthropist found dead. Foul play suspected."

Simon interrupted before Angela could read it, "As you can see, it has already made the paper." He had been surprised at how quickly they had managed to get the story out.

"Philip was a well respected and influential man in this town. He was a kind of celebrity, if you will. He has done a lot for the people of this community over the years. Joe Average makes the big time. The press is going to be all over this, and I'm afraid, they are going to be all over you, as well."

There was concern on his face as he gestured to the man standing silently beside him, "This is Dave Ramsey. He's a criminal lawyer. I've asked him to sit in. As you know, I practice business law. Criminal law is not my forte. Dave is one of the best."

Angela thought. "Why do I need a criminal lawyer? I didn't do anything wrong? What's Mr. Bonder...Simon, so afraid of?"

Dave approached Angela and Elaine smiling, hand outstretched. Then looking specifically at Angela said, "Simon has told me something of your situation. I would like to hear everything that has happened, Angela, if you don't mind. Be as thorough and blunt as you can. It's very important. Tell me everything, no matter how insignificant you may think it is."

Angela nodded her head, and thought, "If I have to tell this story one more time I'm going to scream." There was no passion or emotion in her voice as she told the story of the past couple days.

Dave nodded his head. "Okay." he started. "So who came to see you this morning?"

Angela replied, "Ah, Detectives Davidson and Williams."

Dave's eyebrows rose slightly as he heard the names, "Davidson. He's a good man. Our paths have crossed on a number of occasions. He's dedicated and very intelligent. That's a good thing. Sometimes you get these lackluster cops that have made up their minds before they have even looked at a single piece of evidence."

Angela remembered how professional Davidson had been and how his partner had seemed considerably less so.

Ramsey continued, "Okay. I think our strategy is simple. You two do nothing. Just carry on with your lives as normal - well, as normal as you can under the circumstances. It's obvious to me that you have nothing to worry about. The police will be coming back to talk to you. You will hear from them either later today or tomorrow. I guarantee it. When they do, don't say anything to them - call me. We can sit down, relay our story, and that will be that." He knew it wasn't going to be that simple, it never was, but he didn't want to worry them anymore than necessary. That was a courtesy on which Simon had insisted. Dave had always felt it was better to get the truth out on the table immediately, it prevents complications later, but he respected Simon and his obvious affection for these two.

The buzzer on the phone sounded and Simon answered, "Oh good, send them in", and looked toward the office door. There was a quick knock and two rather large gentlemen breached the doorway. Simon smiled and stood up. Elaine and Angela turned to see who was entering. The two men with their heavy weight body builder physiques looked very hard and intimidating in white crew-neck t-shirts and dark suit jackets. In their presence, the office felt smaller.

Simon spoke proudly, "Ladies, I would like you to meet Joe Smith and Bill Saunders. They will be accompanying you for the next few weeks."

Both Angela and Elaine spun in their chairs and looked at Simon, stunned. Angela spoke first, "What? Bodyguards?" Her voice didn't attempt to conceal her surprise.

Simon was confused, "Well yes, Angela, bodyguards. I told you, Philip was a celebrity in this town. The press is going to be all over you. These gentlemen will be there to make sure things don't get out of hand. We've solicited their services on a number of occasions to protect our clients. They are very good at what they do. You can trust them completely."

Angela had never thought of Philip as a "celebrity" in all the time she had known him. He was just Philip. However, sitting in this office listening to Simon, she realized that many people probably did see him as a celebrity and Simon was probably right. She realized suddenly that she was thinking of Philip as if he were still alive and a quick shiver rushed through her body.

Simon spoke, "Angela, are you still with us?"

She looked up at him and smiled, "Sorry, Mr. Bonder. So much has happened. I guess I'm still reeling from it all."

Simon smiled thoughtfully, "As I was saying, these gentlemen will accompany you everywhere you go. I hope that is all right?"

Angela nodded, and smiled. She got up and introduced herself to them. She looked both men in the eye as she shook their hands. Both men were well over six feet tall and her hand seemed to disappear in theirs.

Angela could hear Simon's voice behind her, "Do whatever they tell you. They are here for your protection, and they know their business very well. Do you understand Angela?" She couldn't imagine anyone being stupid enough not to follow their directions and she nodded.

Simon turned to Elaine, his voice was more compassionate. "That goes for you too, Elaine."

Elaine looked up at Simon, "Me?" she was shaking her head, "No way Simon. I've got far too much to do. I can't have these... I can't have them walking in my shadow." She was noticeably angry.

Simon came around the desk and took Elaine's hands in his, "Trust me about this, Elaine. I know you're a strong woman. Things are going to happen over the next few weeks that… Well, I really don't think you completely understand how bad it is going to be. You will not have a minute of privacy. Someone or other will be sticking a microphone in your face everywhere you go, morning and night. We've seen this a hundred times before. Your life isn't your own right now. You are news, and the media will be relentless. You need these guys, believe me."

Elaine looked into Simon's eyes. She felt something she hadn't felt in a great many years - she was in love. She knew Simon wasn't some over-protective man, he was simply doing what he felt was in her best interest. She could see it in his eyes, and hear it in his voice. She trusted him like she had trusted no one in a very long time. She nodded in agreement without saying another word.

Simon patted the top of her hand lovingly. He was glad she had agreed without too much fuss. "I think we are done here for now. These gentlemen will escort you home. Dave will follow you in his own car. You can be sure the press is all over your front lawn by now. You two just go straight into the house. Dave will give them a statement. Try and stay in the house as much as possible." He looked at Elaine directly. "I would really prefer that you not go to the office until this is over. Can you do that?"

Elaine thought for a few seconds. She wanted to argue, but decided against it. "Yes, my computer at home is connected to the network. Everything else I can do by phone." She thought to herself carefully and then nodded, "Yes. It can be done."

She looked directly at Simon, "As long as it doesn't go on too long. I have a lot at stake. I can't be away for long." She had been in total control of everything in her life for many years and didn't like the feeling of being dependent and vulnerable.

Simon's eyebrows rose slightly as he turned away from them, "I hope it isn't too long, but I can't say for sure."

Elaine sensed how desperately he wanted to give her guarantees, but he simply couldn't and she understood. Standing, she took Angela's hand, "Okay, dear. I think it's time we put these gentlemen to work." She let out a sigh and they left.

* * * * *

Even after Simon's warning, as their car rounded the bend and they saw the house, Elaine gasped, "My God!" The sheer mass of people was almost unbelievable. They now understood the full meaning of Simon's words. Seeing all those people at the house was unnerving and terrifying. They finally realized exactly how much things were about to change.

Dave was in the lead car. Smith was driving their car with Saunders beside him. Saunders turned to face Elaine and Angela. His face was cold, impassionate, and calm. When he spoke, the women felt the involuntary shivers one feels after a clap of thunder, "Okay, ladies.

Here we go. We will wait for Ramsey to get out and distract the press."

He looked at Angela on the passenger side, "Lock your door, Mrs. Evans. When we stop, Smith and I will get out and move to the driver's side of the car. Wait until we open the back door and then both of you get out that side. We'll shield you into the house." He paused and looked at Smith then back to the women, "Don't panic. Just follow our lead. Stick close, and this will be easy. Got it?" and he turned to face the front without waiting for an answer.

After that things happened pretty fast. Anyone trying to get close to the ladies was brushed aside. The two men were forceful and gentle at the same time and Angela and Elaine were very glad these two men were on their side.

Once inside both men smiled as they brushed themselves off. Smith looked at Angela and her mother and saw the distress on their faces. "Are you two okay?" They both smiled and he nodded in acknowledgment. Smith and Saunders proceeded to do the rounds of the house, making sure everything was locked and secure.

The sudden ringing of the phone startled both women. They looked at each other and laughed. Elaine answered it, "Hello, Janet. Yes, she's right here. Hang on."

Angela took the phone, "Hi, Janet. How...?"

Janet interrupted her, "What the hell is going on, Ange? I saw the paper. I've been trying to reach you all day. The cops were here earlier." Her voice was shaky; she was scared.

Angela didn't know what to say to her friend. So much has happened. What could she say? She had to say something. "Philip is dead - murdered. The police don't know who yet." Angela's voice sounded cold. She knew it but couldn't stop herself. "Can you come?"

The phone went dead.

Elaine looked at Angela as she hung up, "Janet's coming, is she?"

Angela nodded, "She'll be here in a few minutes."

Elaine headed to the kitchen to put on some tea.

Elaine liked Janet. Of all the friends Angela had, Janet was special to her. She knew what people thought of her, but she had always seen her as a warm, caring individual. She had always thought it such a waste for Janet to feel the need to portray herself as the dumb blonde. She knew that Janet was much more.

Before long Janet arrived. Smith and Saunders saw her car pull up and went out to help her in. Once in the house she headed straight for the living room. "Jesus Christ, Ange! You could have warned me!"

Angela looked up, and smiled apologetically. "Sorry dear. I've had a few things on my mind lately." and she shook her head.

Janet chuckled, "Ordinarily, I would love to have that many men pawing at me, but shit. And what's with the two gorillas."

Angela patted the cushion beside her, "Sit."

Janet complied and poured herself a cup of the tea. "Well?"

Angela hesitated before she spoke, "Philip's been murdered. The police think I may have had something to do with it."

Janet looked at her, "I know. They were by my place. They asked all kinds of questions about you and Philip. I was so scared. I told them everything about his affairs, and your fight - everything." She remembered how the interview had seemed more like an interrogation,

"Maybe I shouldn't have told them anything. Damn, Angela. I'm sorry."

Angela smiled to comfort her friend and took a sip of her tea. "You did the right thing, Jan. I don't have anything to hide."

Janet's forehead formed a deep frown, "But, Angela, it looks so bad."

Angela nodded, "It does. I think the thing to remember is that they have to be able to prove that I did it. I'm innocent until proven guilty. Since I didn't do it, they can't. So it doesn't matter how it looks, I'm okay."

Janet smiled thinking maybe Angela was experiencing some kind of delusional fantasy. She didn't believe for one second that her girlfriend had nothing to worry about. She looked around the room and noticed Smith and Saunders standing in the foyer again. Angela knew what Janet was looking at, "They're Mr. Bonder's idea. They're here to protect Mom and me."

Janet snickered, "No shit." She shook her head, and looked back at Angela. She had a devilish smile on her face, and made no attempt to lower her voice. "Can you imagine those guys in the sack? It'd be like being run over by a steam roller or something."

It made Angela laugh hard. How totally inappropriate of Janet, she thought and was glad of the bit of levity.

Angela changed the subject, "How's Mike?"

The smile left Janet's face and she looked down at her feet for a second, then back at Angela, "We split up. We had a big fight."

Angela reached for her hand, "Oh, Janet. I'm so sorry. I thought things were good between you two."

Janet's smile was pitiful, "No big deal. He's a pig. I don't know what I was thinking. It was okay while it lasted."

Angela could see her friend's hurt. Clearly her feelings for him had been deep. "What happened?" Angela asked, already knowing the answer.

Janet replied, "That asshole had the nerve to give me shit for telling you about Philip. I lost it. I went ballistic on him." She thought to herself, remembering every detail of their fight. She shrugged her shoulders, "I can't be with someone like that. Someone who thinks secrets like that should be kept. He wanted me to keep secrets from you." She paused for a second. She had decided that the breakup was for the best. "Ah, to hell with him. I don't need that shit." She shook her head, looked back at Angela, then laughed, "What a pair of sorry asses we are." She paused, "Don't worry Angela. We'll get through this. Life is good, we're good. We don't deserve this. Everything will work out. It always does."

Angela thought how special her friend truly was. In the midst of all this, she continued to say we, as if she was in the same predicament. It was Angela's problem but Janet made no distinction. Her friend was in trouble and therefore she was in trouble as well. Nothing ever happened to one that the other wasn't somehow involved.

"Speaking of which, did I tell you that I saw Lisa the other day?" Janet wasn't deliberately changing the subject. Recalling the meeting just came to mind, "She has a new boyfriend. He is some kind of computer geek or something. I haven't met him yet, but Lisa sure seemed happy. She said he was going to be rich. You know Lisa! She's always looking for that pot of gold."

Angela realized that she hadn't talked to Lisa since the wedding. However, she was pleased that her friend had someone special in her life. It was good to hear of someone enjoying happier times. Angela responded with a smile, "I am so happy for her. She deserves it. After the things she has been through in her life, she certainly could use a little happiness." She paused for a second then added, "It's nice to hear someone is happy."

18

The Lieutenant stood in the door of his office looking over the organized confusion of the squad room. He saw Williams and Davidson talking over the coffee pot and yelled to them. "Williams. Davidson. In here, now!"

They turned to the familiar voice and casually strolled over to the office. Sam knew full well what was about to happen. The Lieutenant wasn't pleased but he simply didn't care - the wife didn't do it!!

Closing the office door behind them, each took a chair facing the Lieutenant's desk. He was reading a file and after several seconds looked up. After considering both men momentarily, his stare settled on Sam. "Okay let's have it. What's happening in the Evan's case?"

Sam shrugged his shoulders. His voice was calm as he spoke, "The investigation is ongoing. We don't have any solid leads yet, but we are on top of it."

Williams' head snapped in total surprise towards his partner. The Lieutenant laughed unpleasantly and sat back in his chair, "I'd say your partner has a different opinion. I do too."

Sam looked at his partner with displeasure before returning his attention to the Lieutenant. "Look, Lieutenant, I know what it looks like. I'm not stupid, but I just know she didn't do this. Someone killed him, that's for sure. It just wasn't her."

The Lieutenant pointed at the file, "Obviously you know something that isn't in here."

Sam looked at the floor to gather his thoughts, "Listen Lieutenant, you weren't there. You didn't see the look in her eyes, or the way she reacted to the news. Just everything about her. There's just no way she did it. I can feel it in my gut."

Williams couldn't stay quiet any longer, "Your gut? Damn it. We can put her at or near the scene at about the right time. They had that big fight. She still had blood on her hands, for Christ sake. He was rich. He'd been screwing around on her. She wouldn't get a penny from him unless he died - the pre-nup saw to that. I mean, damn it man, it's the oldest story in the book. She got pissed off, popped him, and then tried to make it look like a suicide. She is one cold, calculating bitch. At the house, she was acting - playing her role as the grieving widow. I've seen it before, damn it. Open and shut."

The Lieutenant didn't like Williams. He was too eager to make a name for himself. Still, the Lieutenant had to agree with him. He looked back at Sam, "Look, Sam. I've known you for a lot of years. Your instincts are almost legendary in this office, but your partner is right. The press is camping out at every exit. Hell, I've even been getting calls from damned concerned citizens wanting to know why we haven't arrested anyone yet. Look Sam, you've got to give me something - anything."

Sam had nothing more to say, so the Lieutenant continued, "Okay. I have no choice." He looked at Williams, "Bring her in."

Williams clapped his hands once, his face displaying a broad smile as he headed for the door.

Sam looked at the Lieutenant, "Christ, it's only been a few hours. Give us a little more time. You know the consequences if we're wrong." He wanted to say something more but just couldn't think what.

Sam remembered first meeting the Lieutenant when they were both rookies. He recalled the Lieutenant telling him that his original plan was to be a lawyer. At college, one of his professors subscribed to the theory that in order to be a good lawyer one needs to see where the client is coming from and he made arrangements for his students to ride with the police on patrol.

The Lieutenant had been stunned by the things he had seen. The experience changed his whole perspective and he gained a new appreciation for the police. He had decided that the front line, rather than the courtroom, was where he wanted to be.

As they left his office, the Lieutenant remembered his days as a detective. Those were the good times. He hated being in an office so totally detached from the real action and the real work. He remembered how he had been virtually forced to take the promotion to Lieutenant. He hated this job - he missed the streets.

* * * * *

Angela, Elaine, and Janet were sitting in front of the fire, laughing and talking as they recounted the memories they had shared over the years. It seemed to them appropriate to be remembering all the good times they had had. So much had gone wrong in their lives lately, they felt a need to relive better times.

Angela appreciated Janet being there, she needed her. It reminded her of who she was and what she meant to people - and what they meant to her. These current events were almost overwhelming, but life would go on eventually.

Smith and Saunders noticed the car in the driveway and were heading out to meet its occupants. When they realized who it was, they stopped. They had a pretty good idea why the detectives had returned and they certainly weren't going to do anything to assist them. They retreated back into the house.

Hearing the doorbell, Angela looked up. Seeing Smith and Saunders, she smiled at them. They returned her smile but made no effort to approach the door. Angela's smile turned to a frown, "Why aren't you answering it?" She got up to go to the door herself.

Saunders put up his hand signaling Angela to stop, "Please, stay back from the door, Mrs. Evans." His voice was forceful and she stopped in her tracks. He continued, "It's the cops. We'll let them in."

He still didn't move and his smile returned. A few more seconds went by before Saunders slowly approached the door. Williams and Sam were standing with their backs to the door and didn't notice it open. Everyone inside the house could hear the reporters yelling questions at the two officers. Saunders started towards the two officers, but stopped as they turned around. He smiled an unnerving smile as he stepped aside to allow them passage.

Williams saw Angela first, "Ah, Mrs. Evans, nice to see you again." He continued into the living room towards her, "We're here to arrest you for the murder of Philip Evans."

Angela was immediately stunned and staggered backwards as if those words had been a physical blow. Janet and Elaine gasped in equal shock. Sam had a very annoyed look on his face and thought, "There must be a hundred different ways to do this and this was probably the worst." He was not at all pleased with his partner.

Angela collected herself and retreated to her mother. Elaine took her in her arms. Williams was still smiling as he reached his hand out to Angela, "Would you come with us please."

Elaine screamed, "No!" Her voice seemed to rumble through the room like the most violent of storms. It startled Williams and he took a step back. "Please, Mrs. Michails, I'm just doing my job." His voice became more forceful as Sam came around the couch in front of them. "Mrs. Evans, please come with us."

Angela stared at the two officers. Her face displayed the terror she was feeling. Sam looked sympathetically back at her. Williams had lost his smile and looked considerably more forceful.

Elaine continued staring at the two officers and when she spoke her voice was a cold, hard whisper. "She didn't do it. I killed the bastard. I did it."

A look of disbelief crossed Sam's face. He stared at Elaine for a second or two then realized what she was doing. He knew that she was about as guilty as Angela and it made him smile. This woman had just endeared herself to him and he chuckled. He walked over to the armchair and sat down. A wide grin lit up his face as he crossed his legs and folded his arms across his chest.

Sam enjoyed nothing better than to take stories apart, look at things the way they seem, dissect them, and then reorganize them into reality. He believed everyone at some point reaches a crossroads. The direction their life takes is determined by one simple little decision - turn left, turn right, or go straight ahead. Everything comes down to simple little decisions - decisions that can change an entire life. He was eager to see this scenario played out.

Williams was stunned by Elaine's sudden outburst and confession. He was equally stunned at his partner's reaction. He looked over at Sam sitting in the chair and was annoyed.

Sam continued to smile as he brushed his hand through the air as if to say, "You wanted this. You've got the floor. Deal with it." He didn't offer a single word of encouragement to his partner, and was determined to sit back and enjoy the show that was about to begin.

Williams gathered himself up before he proceeded. "All right, Mrs. Michails. Let's hear it. I suppose you want a lawyer present."

Elaine shook her head. She was determined that these officers weren't going to be taking her daughter anywhere.

Angela looked at her mother in shock. "No, Mom. Don't do this. I can't let you do this."

Elaine pushed her daughter aside gently and got up, "Shut up, Angela." Her voice was calm. Janet's eyes were darting between Angela, Elaine, and the two detectives. She had no idea what was going on.

Elaine walked over to the fire and stared into it as she gathered her thoughts. She knew her story would have to be convincing. "I came home that night and Angela wasn't here. I saw the answering machine all smashed and I knew something terrible must have happened. I knew Angela usually told everything to Janet, so I thought if anyone knew what was going on, she would. So I gave her a call." Sam looked over at Janet to see if there was any reaction. She still carried the dazed look on her face as she nodded the validity of the statement, and he chuckled quietly when he saw it.

"I was right, of course. Janet told me everything about Philip's affairs, her father's leaving - all of it. I was so totally enraged at Philip." She paused to reflect and chuckled to herself. "It's really quite amazing how easy it is to buy a gun when you want one. It felt heavy in my hands." She paused for effect, holding her hands as if a gun were in them.

"I had decided that it was best if it looked like a suicide. I came back here and typed a letter on the computer. I was sure it would be convincing. Then I phoned Philip and pleaded with him to meet me at the beach. I told him that I wanted to talk about Angela and him. He agreed to meet me." She paused again.

"When I got to the beach, Philip was sitting in his car looking out at the ocean. I walked over and opened the door. I just looked at him for a second. He looked smug and wounded at the same time. I pulled out the letter and tossed it across him into the car. I saw him watch it go by. The gun was in my hand then. I don't remember pulling it out but there it was. Something must have caught his eye because just then he spun around and was looking down the barrel. I hesitated long enough for him to realize what was about to happen, then I pulled the trigger." She took a deep breath and sighed. It was done. She hoped it was convincing. She stood silently for a few seconds then turned to face the room.

Everyone looked stunned - everyone that is except Sam. When Elaine looked directly at him, he winked. It was obvious that he didn't believe a word of it. She tried to think where she may have gone wrong.

Sam was impressed with her story and under different circumstances, he might have believed it. He fought the urge to stand up and applaud. He knew the facts and this story was as wrong as it could possibly be.

Williams looked confused as his eyes darted back and forth between Elaine and Angela. He didn't know what to believe. All the evidence they had gathered pointed squarely at Angela, but the story her mother had relayed was just as plausible. He looked at Sam who smiled, "So what are you going to do now?"

Sam was enjoying this. He could see Williams had been taken in by the story. It hadn't even occurred to him that she may be making it all up. Sam almost felt sorry for him.

Angela was dumbfounded as she looked at her mother. She was trying hard not to believe her story but it had been pretty convincing. Still, she had trouble believing her mother could do such a thing. Angela now wished she had woken her that night to talk. She would know at this moment whether or not Elaine had actually been home.

Sam was still looking at his partner, "Well? Where do we go from here?"

Williams wasn't really sure what he should do and was annoyed at Sam's total lack of support. "Well, I think we had better take both of them in and try to sort this out."

Angela stood up as if on cue and joined her mother. Escorted by Williams they started out of the house to the car.

Janet was getting up as well thinking for some reason she should join them. Sam put up his hand to stop her and walked over to talk to her.

Williams looked over his shoulder and saw his partner, "You coming?"

Sam looked back him, "Ah... No. You go ahead. I'm sure Janet here would be happy to give me a ride in."

Janet was going to say something in protest but Sam had put his finger to his lips. Williams shrugged his shoulders and continued outside. Smith and Saunders followed them. They were determined to continue to do their job and cleared a path for the three to the officer's car. Saunders decided he and Smith would drive Elaine's car to the police station. They would call Mr. Bonder on the way to inform him of the latest developments. Once they had left Sam, continued his conversation with Janet.

19

The Lieutenant spotted Sam sitting at his desk and made his way to him through the chaos of officers and their wards. Mounted on one of the pillars was a television tuned to the local news channel. The Lieutenant could hear it but wasn't paying any attention. He reached Sam just as he was finishing his telephone conversation, "Thank you. You've been very helpful." Hanging up he noticed the Lieutenant, "Hey, have I got..."

"I just saw your partner downstairs," yelled the Lieutenant, interrupting Sam. "You brought in the Evans woman, her mother, a pack of lawyers… Hell there's even a couple circus rejects down there. What the hell is going on?"

Sam chuckled imagining the scene, "How's my partner making out anyway?"

The Lieutenant wanted to laugh thinking of Williams dealing with it all, but he was too angry. "He's running around like a blind dog chasing his own fart. Why aren't you down there with him?"

Sam continued smiling, "You should have been there, it was great. Williams goes strutting into the house, ready to bring in his man. He starts telling Evans that he's arresting her, and dear old Mom pipes up and confesses to the whole damn thing." Sam shook his head. "I wanted to applaud. It was great."

"I'm not amused, Sam!" barked the Lieutenant.

Sam puts up his hand, "Sorry. Her performance was brilliant, though. Hell, if I didn't know any better I'd say she actually did it."

The Lieutenant frowned, "So what are you saying? It was a conspiracy. They're both in it together?"

Sam's smile vanished. "Shit, Lieutenant. Those women are about as guilty as I am." He paused to reflect. "Listen. When Williams left with them I had a nice little chat with Mrs. Evans' girlfriend. Remember Janet?"

The Lieutenant nodded, "Yeah, Yeah... in the report."

Sam continued, "Well, it turns out Janet knows everything that goes on in Evans' life. Hell, if you what to know the last time Evans took a piss, ask Janet."

Seeing the Lieutenant's impatience, Sam continued, "Anyway, it seems Janet was sleeping with the best friend of our dearly departed. Our Mr. Evans shared everything he did with this Mike character. Mike and Janet seemed to spend a lot of their time talking about Mr. and Mrs. Evans." He was laughing again. "This whole thing sounds like a God damned soap opera." and shook his head. "Anyway, it boils down to this, if you want to know anything about the world of Angela and Philip just ask the encyclopedia, Janet."

Although he would prefer to do without the theatrics, the Lieutenant was beginning to think Sam's take on the situation might be leading somewhere. "Okay, you've got my attention. Go on."

Sam was pleased, "So anyway. It turns out Mrs. Evans had two fathers. The first one her mother married. He died some fifteen years ago – bad ticker, worked himself to death or something. The second was her biological father. She's a bloody sperm bank baby!" Disappointed by the lack of response, Sam continued, "Anyway, Mrs. Evans decides she wants to find her long lost gene pool. She hires a P.I., and he tracks down Daddy number two. Apparently the old boy had been through some real shit in his life. When Mr. Evans finds out about him, he forbids Mrs. Evans to see him anymore. Mrs. Evans tells this to her father, one John Simmons. He goes a little nuts - he wasn't what you'd call a rock anyway. He decides it's too much for him and he just heads for the hills."

The Lieutenant was getting bored, "So who cares…the old boy takes off, so what?"

Sam smiles at him, "Mrs. Evans had her little chat with him the night before the murder. He made it look like he left town the day of the murder. I was talking to an Andrea - one of Simmons' co-workers, and after dropping one of the hotel guests at the airport, who do you think she sees get on a domestic? None other than our friend, Mr. Simmons. That was the day after the murder." Sam was pleased with this scenario.

The implication was clear but the Lieutenant wasn't as yet prepared to get excited. "So the old man had a few loose ends to tidy up before he left. That doesn't make him a murderer."

Sam sat back in his chair, "There's more. Janet tells me that Mr. Evans had taken a business trip a few weeks back. He had picked up some bimbo in the hotel bar and went back to her room for a little horizontal aerobics. Interestingly, Simmons' flight destination was that very same town."

The Lieutenant stood silently for a few moments, reviewing the information: innuendo, hear say, and coincidence – no solid evidence about anything. "Sam, it all sounds wonderful, but let's face it, you still don't have shit. I've got a circus act downstairs and enough to charge. None of that has changed."

Sam was angry and more than a little disgusted that his superior couldn't see the obvious. "Ah, come on Lieutenant, you know damn well there's enough here to cause reasonable doubt that either of the women had anything to do with the murder. Quit waving the book in my face. Let me run with this. Cut them loose… Say it was routine questioning or something. I need some time."

The Lieutenant was about to say something when the television caught his attention. "'Black Widow arrested. That story and more after this important message from our sponsors."

Hearing those words the Lieutenant looked down at Davidson. "Now what am I going to do? Those bastards are already on this… All right, run with it. You don't have a lot of time. What the hell am I going to say to the media?" It was a rhetorical question.

Sam got up smiling, "That's what you get the big bucks for, Boss. I have a plane to catch." He gave the Lieutenant a friendly slap on the shoulder as he walked by.

Then Sam stopped, "You are going to cut them loose?"

The Lieutenant thought for a second, and then nodded. He looked hard into Sam's face, "Yeah. They're out of here. You have 24 hours to bring me something solid, or I'll have no choice."

Sam knew what he meant. He also knew how tough his own job was about to become. "You'll take care of Williams for me?" He laughed out loud at that.

The Lieutenant laughed back, "Yeah. I think the poor shit could use a day off."

* * * * *

Williams was in the middle of a question when the Lieutenant walked in. Angela, Elaine, and the lawyers were sitting on one side of the long table and Williams was on the other.

The Lieutenant's face was cold and emotionless as he spoke, "You're free to go."

Williams' jaw dropped, "What are you talking 'bout? Ah, sir" The Lieutenant looked down at him with an expression that clearly said, "Shut up."

Ramsey responded, sounding confused, "Excuse me?"

The Lieutenant looked at him, "That's all we need for now. You can go. We'll be in touch."

Ramsey became annoyed, "You drag us down here. Flat out accuse us of murder and now it's 'Oops, sorry, bye.' I think you have some explaining to do."

The Lieutenant looked Ramsey in the eye, "Let there be no mistake. I'm not in the least sorry. You're clients are still my number one choice. This investigation is ongoing. I'm allowing your clients to go, cuz I'm a nice guy. If you prefer, I'd be happy to process them, book the pair of them for conspiracy to commit and let you prove in court we were wrong. It's your call counselor." He wasn't kidding, he would do it. The past few days had worn his patience thin.

Ramsey had crossed paths with the Lieutenant before and he knew when to push and when to back off. This was clearly a "back off" situation. He thought quickly of the grief and torment Angela and Elaine had already suffered. He knew it would be nothing compared to what they would go through if they were actually booked. His voice was calm and sincere, "Thank you, Lieutenant. We want this case resolved as much as you do. If there is anything our office can do to help, please don't hesitate to call."

The Lieutenant smiled at the lip service, appreciated it anyway. "Thank you." He reached down and tapped Williams on the shoulder and motioned him to follow. Williams was still angry and needed the satisfaction of a complete explanation.

When they were clear of the interrogation room, Williams stopped and grabbed the Lieutenant's elbow. "Excuse me, sir!" His voice was less than respectful. "But just what the hell is going on!?"

The Lieutenant stopped and turned to Williams. "I'm still your superior. I don't have to explain myself to you."

Williams didn't let up, "Yeah! I think you do, sir! This is a good case? Don't you think I have a right to know? And where the hell is my partner through all this? Why isn't he here?"

The Lieutenant softened his tone, "Look. Sam came up with some new information that might prove that those ladies in there had nothing to do with this. I'm not prepared to go into it with you. I trust him. If he chose not to share with you, I respect that." Personally, he thought it was very bad form for Sam not to include his partner in all aspects of this investigation. "Look. You've got a stack of files on your desk. Work on those 'til Sam gets back. Okay?"

Williams had more to say but the Lieutenant walked away leaving him standing there fuming.

* * * * *

Once back at the house, they made their way through the mob scene on the lawn to the front door. The reporters were becoming more aggressive and Angela seemed to snap. A look of cold strength replaced the look of terror. At the door she turned to face the crowd gathered around her. She glanced over the reporters who were yelling their questions at her. It was a cacophony.

She realized they weren't at all like sharks in a feeding frenzy. Instead, she thought they were more like Oliver in the dining hall begging, "Please, sir, I want some more?" She now pitied them. They no longer intimidated or scared her.

Everyone was in the living room. Elaine was sitting on the couch with Janet. Ramsey and Bonder were standing in front of them offering comfort. Smith and Saunders had taken up vigil at the front window. They each had a section of the drapes in their hand, pulled back slightly to see through.

Angela sauntered in smiling and then started to laugh. Her mother was unnerved by its unusual sound and looked at Angela with concern. Angela clapped her hands, and rubbed them back and forth as she headed toward the small bar, "Well, that certainly was a lot of fun."

She reached for the bottle of Scotch and poured herself a drink and downed it in one motion. She gasped as she looked at the label, “Ballentines. Good shit." She poured herself another. Taking a smaller sip she observed the shocked faces on the others as they watched her, mesmerized. She laughed at the sight of them. She held the bottle in front of her. "Can I interest anyone in a snort?" Hearing no response, she shrugged, put the bottle back, and joined her mother.

Elaine watched her daughter's approach in disbelief. This wasn't her daughter. It was her body, but there was someone else in it. Angela sat close and looked into her mother's eyes. "So, Mom? Whatcha think? We gonna fry?" She laughed and took another sip.

Elaine didn't know what to say or do. Her hand shot up and slapped Angela's cheek, hard. It had surprised her as much as Angela. Angela's cheek was immediately red and the impression of Elaine's fingers showed in contrast to the red. Angela grabbed for her face in shock. Elaine realized what she had done and pulled her daughter into a strong embrace. Angela resisted for a second, then she dropped her glass to the floor and returned the hug. Angela began to cry uncontrollably. Elaine knew what was happening to her daughter. She knew Angela would never be the same again. At that thought, Elaine started to cry as well. The two men looked at each other dumfounded and took it as a cue. The Scotch suddenly seemed like a good idea and they headed for the bar.

Smith and Saunders watched the two women embracing on the couch. They saw Simon and Ramsey retreat towards the bar and they decided to leave the room.

20

Sam's flight arrived on time. He had discovered that Mr. Simmons had a sister living here and that would be his starting point - tomorrow. Tonight, he just wanted to get to the hotel and go to sleep. The flight had been smooth and uneventful, but he always felt anxious when flying - such an unnatural way to travel.

Sam never took vacations, preferring instead to stay at home when he had time off. The thought of exploring the world had no appeal. His day to day routine was all the adventure he wanted. When he did have time off, he spent this precious free time locked behind closed doors watching old movies or reading books. If the weather was particularly nice he would take long walks on the beach. Mostly, he just wanted to escape humanity.

He often thought how vicious his species was. Animals are motivated by the basic needs of survival. For mankind, the motivators were always the emotions - greed, lust, jealousy, or revenge.

He shook his head, flying always initiated these strange thoughts in him. He grabbed his suitcase off the carousel and headed out of the terminal through a sea of stressed out people. He smiled to himself, "What a pleasant way to travel." Outside the cabs were lined up waiting to serve.

* * * * *

He woke early, and glanced at his watch as he put it on. He had left a wake up call with the desk for 7:00 a.m. – just in case. He chuckled, "I'll be showered, shaved, and finished breakfast by seven." Rubbing the sleep from his eyes, he started for the shower.

All through his morning ritual and his breakfast, the only thing on his mind was the case - Angela, Elaine, Simmons, and Philip. How did it all fit? What was the link? Who was guilty? What was the motivation here? No matter what it took, today he would find out. Today he would have the answers.

* * * * *

"Wanna nuther one?" she asked as she stood beside the table with the coffee pot poised. John looked up at his sister and smiled. "Thanks, I'd love one. You certainly make great coffee."

She smiled with a hint of pride on her face. John felt love looking at her in her housecoat and pink fuzzy slippers. He thought back to his own wife and tried to imagine her standing here instead of his sister. It made his heart heavy thinking about all the things that had gone wrong all those years ago. He wanted to cry but he smiled instead, "I can't tell you how good it is to see you. I really needed to see you. Thanks for letting me come."

Growing up, they had had a typical brother/sister relationship. They fought and bickered as siblings do. She was older by two years and he loved her. She was his sister and he had always protected her. It had been his obligation and his duty, whether or not she needed it.

When they had grown and gone their separate ways, they lost touch. Even during his bad times, he did not contact her. He wished now that he had come to her before everything fell apart. Maybe things would have turned out differently.

She was smiling as she sat across from him. "Jim and I are very glad to have you. He has wanted to meet you for a very long time. We didn't know how to reach you, but after what you told us last night, I know why. I really wish you had called us back then. We would have been there for you." The smile on her face didn't mask her sorrow.

John's wife had called back then and told her everything. She remembered how scared and helpless she felt. She had done nothing and now she felt guilty. She would never admit to him how much she had known or how helpless she had felt. She needed to change the subject. It was time to move on. "So, tell me more about Angela. What's she like?"

The thought of Angela brought a warm smile to his face "Ah, she's the greatest. She has grown into such a special woman. My only regret is that I didn't see her grow up. She showed me all kinds of photos and things. She's married now." He hesitated there, thinking of Philip and the things he had said. "He's a jerk, her husband...a real prize. He has forbidden her to see me you know." He took a sip of his coffee. "I was so hurt, so angry. He had no right to take her away from me." His eyes showed the hate he was feeling. He recognized it and fought back. "I don't know what I'm going to do. Now that I have met her, seen her, been with her, I know I have to make her a part of my life." He was still trying to think of a way to get Philip to change his mind, "I had to get out of there, or I would have done something I would regret. I've been down that road before." He looked at his sister for a few seconds before continuing. "That's why I came. I needed to get some balance. Think things through." He took another sip. "I know I'm going to go back there. I know it. I will confront Philip. I know I can get through to him. I just need some time."

She believed him and knew this time it would be different. This time she would be there for him. Her eyes wandered around the kitchen as she thought about her own life. Her own two children were now grown and out in the world. She hoped they would have the sense to stay in touch and hold onto the special love of family. She hoped they would never be exposed to the emptiness of being physically and spiritually alone. No matter what feelings they had, what differences developed, or what disputes occurred, she hoped they would always know that family is the only thing that really matters.

Her eye caught the clock on the wall, "My God, would you look at that. 10:00 a.m. and I'm not even dressed. Where does the time go?" She felt she should be dressed and ready for the day by seven thirty – every day. She was glad to have these few days off. "Have another cup of coffee if you'd like. I've got to get some clothes on. Maybe later we can go shopping or lunch or something - whatever you want." She smiled sincerely.

He took another sip of his coffee and looked back at her. "I'd like that." He hated shopping and secretly hoped she would come up with something else for them to do. All he really wanted was to get reacquainted with her and make up for all the time that had passed.

John's thoughts often returned to his parents but this was the first time he actually missed them. He wished he had known about the funeral; he would have liked to say good-bye. He remembered where he was at that time and the memory disgusted him.

The doorbell rang just as Jill stepped out of the kitchen. Stopping, she looked down at herself, "Damn. Who could that be?" She brushed her hands across the front of her housecoat and tried to fix her hair as she walked down the hall. Realizing the futility, she cursed under her breath and opened the door, "Yes?"

Sam smiled politely as he handed her his card, "Mrs. Jill Malcolm?" He knew it was her, asking only as a formality. She stared at his card in her hand, "That's right? What can I do for you?"

Sam's expression never changed, "Do you know where I might find John Simmons?"

Hearing his name, John got up and started toward the door, "I'm John Simmons. What can I do for you?"

Sam's eyes left Jill and went to John. He held his own expression while noting the look of surprise and curiosity on John's face. He believed it was real, "Eyes are the windows to the soul". Sam knew this initial contact was critically important. He believed he could tell what was going through someone's mind at this point. The look he saw in John was that of genuine curiosity and he thought, "First point in his favor."

Sam knew his next task would be to test this man's credibility. He would ask John questions to which he already had the answers. This would establish a base. Sam liked this part of the interview.

He reached into his pocket and pulled out another card and handed it towards John. "May I come in?"

John took the card and looked at his sister, then looked back at Sam, "Sure, why not?" and led the way back to the kitchen.

John pointed to one of the chairs inviting Sam to sit, "Would you like a coffee..." He looked at the card again, "Detective Davidson?"

Sam looked at him thoughtfully, "Thank you. I'd love one." He pulled his note pad from his shirt pocket as he sat down.

With the coffee delivered, John sat across from Sam. Jill, whose curiosity was greater than her desire to get dressed, joined the men at the table. Sam deliberately took his time, wanting the anxiety and curiosity to build. He was observing their nervousness as he took a long sip from his cup. It was point two in their favor. The guilty, too, were always nervous, but it was a different kind of nervousness. He had seen it many times and could easily tell the difference.

It was time, "So, Mr. Simmons. How long have you been in town?"

John looked at him. The question startled him. Not the question itself, just the fact that he had finally asked one. "Ah... A couple of days"

John fought to remember which specific day he had arrived. Sam noticed him fighting to recall and thought, “Point three,” and nodded his acknowledgment. "Jill here, she's your sister?"

John nodded, his eyebrows raised slightly as he looked curiously at his sister, "Ah yeah. Why?"

Sam shook his head slightly, like the question and answer didn't mean anything other than polite conversation.

John was anxious, "Can you tell me what this is all about? Why are you here?"

“Point four,” Sam thought. His choreographed interview style always gave him the information he wanted. He was beginning to think John was innocent. "John, do you know an Angela Evans?" He focused hard on John, wanting him to see it. So far John was displaying all the typical emotional transitions the innocent go through when confronted with an implied accusation.

John looked worried, "Angela? What's happened? Is she okay?" his anxiety was peaking.

Sam’s voice was calm. "Angela? Yeah, she's fine."

Sam knew she was probably going through her own little hell at this very moment but in the context of this conversation, she was okay. He paused to let John absorb that information before continuing. "What about her husband, Philip? Know him?"

John's heart raced, anxiously wondering where all this was heading. He was getting angry. "Yes, damn it. I know him. Well, rather I know of him. I've never actually met him. What the hell is going on?"

Sam became relaxed. He was confident John had passed his tests and now considered him innocent. He had hoped he could wrap up this case here and now, but it was clear that someone else had committed the murder. He did allow some compassion, "I'm afraid Philip is dead - murdered."

Suddenly John realized why this cop was here. "You think I did it, don't you? That's why you are here, isn't it?"

Sam took a thoughtful sip of his coffee and replaced it on the table. He looked John square in the eye, "Frankly, Mr. Simmons, yes. I was sure you were involved. Maybe even that you did it. I don't think that anymore. I believe you're innocent and frankly, that kinda pisses me off. That means the killer is still out there." It was his last test for John. The look of shock and relief he saw in his face was all he needed.

John relaxed somewhat, "Angela? My god, how's she doing?"

Sam thought carefully. It wasn't really his place to make emotional assessments, "Frankly John, she's going through hell. She's the prime suspect in this murder. My superiors believe they have enough to indict. Personally, I think she is about as guilty as I am. I'm trying to find the real killer before this goes too far."

John looked hard at Sam and saw he cared about Angela. He felt grateful for that. The urge to help was strong, but he simply didn't know Philip and Angela well enough to be helpful.

Sam continued, "On your flight here you were sitting beside a young woman. What can you tell me about her?"

"Oh yeah, Lisa… Lisa.... Lisa.... Lisa Douglas" I don't really know her. We met on the plane. She was coming here for a couple of days and then she was heading down to Mexico. It sounded to me like she was here on business or something and then going on a vacation." John paused for a moment, "She told me the name of the company she worked for…" He searched his memory and then said the name.

That caught Sam's attention, "You do realize Mr. Evans owned that company." Sam was excited again, "I really need to find her. I have some questions I would like to ask her."

John was shocked, he hadn't known the name of the Philip's company or that she was his employee. Suddenly, things she had said started making sense. He felt he now had information this cop would like to hear.

"There were a few things she said that didn't really make a lot of sense to me at the time. I just thought she was a little off. It really sounded like it was business and then a vacation, but after what you just said..." He thought for a second and knew it was more.

Sam pushed, "Yes. Whatever you have, I want to hear it. It could be important."

John was shaking his head, "I don't know. It just may be coincidence..."

Sam thought, "There's that word again, coincidence. What are the odds of her being on the same flight as John and sitting next to him? It has to be more than a coincidence."

John continued, "She was mentioning how pissed she had been with her boss. He owed her money. It sounded like it had been for quite awhile. She had confronted him. It sounded like she got it because she said that she had really shown him. That's the way she put it, 'I really showed him', and now she was going on this long vacation. She had also mentioned some boyfriend, or at least he sounded like he was her boyfriend. He had gotten in her way, wanted too much from her. He sounded like he was one of those needy, clingy types. She said how she had wanted to kill him. To me, it sounded like a figure of speech. I mean, how many times have I said, 'I'm going to kill so and so'. We all say it, we never mean it literally. Now after this, I'm not so sure about her."

Sam's heart started to race. "She didn't say where she was staying or anything like that, did she?" Hoping beyond hope she had.

John smiled a knowing smile, "As a matter of fact she did. I mean she looked like a motel kind of a gal to me but she said she was going to be staying at the Regency. It was like she was bragging about it or something. It was what made me think that she was here on business. That perhaps the company she worked for was going to be footing the bill. She said she had friends here, and that she would be seeing them while in town, then off to Mexico."

Sam was feeling hope again. Lisa had just become a very interesting individual. He would have to meet with her face to face, and then he would know.

John noticed Sam's face. It was obvious this cop was pleased with the information he had just given him. "Does that help?"

Sam smiled, and nodded, "Yes. I'd say that was very useful. May I borrow your phone?"

Jill pointed towards the living room. Sam saw the telephone and the phone book clearly visible underneath and went to it. He quickly located the number and punched it into the keypad on the phone.

After the second ring a voice responded, "Good Morning. Regency Hotel, Diane speaking. How may I help you?"

It was the voice of an angel. "Yes, good morning, Diane. This is Detective Davidson. Do you have a guest registered under the name of Lisa Douglas?" There was no reason for him to think she would have registered under a different name.

Diane responded professionally. He was sure the hotel had trained their employees carefully in the handling of telephone calls. "Lisa Douglas?" She paused. Sam was hoping she was doing the search. He could hear only muffled conversation through the phone. It wasn't long before she came back on the line "Yes Detective Davidson. She is a guest here."

"Please, don't let her leave before I get there. It's extremely important that I see her. Do you understand? I'm only a few minutes away. I'll be there in...." he looked at Jill. She understood and held up five fingers. "I'll be there in five minutes. Please, this is very important."

There was no response from the other end of the phone. Sam could hear the murmur of people talking in the background, and the faint tap of a computer keyboard. After what seemed an eternity, Diane spoke. Her voice almost a whisper, she was obviously trying to ensure no one heard her. "Yes Detective. I should be able to do that."

Sam smiled. She had just told him Lisa was still there and she hadn't called down to check out. "Thank you, Diane. I'll be there as quickly as I can."

Abandoning the couch, he started for the door. He paused momentarily and looked back at the surprised faces of John and Jill. "Thank you. You have been very helpful." Then his eyes moved specifically toward John, "I will call you, and let you know what happens, okay?" John smiled and nodded. Then Sam smiled at Jill. "Thank you for the coffee. I can honestly say it was the best coffee I can remember." Jill was pleased but thought it strange for him to mention it. She dismissed it as simple jubilance.

* * * * *

It had taken Sam more than the five minutes to reach the hotel. He shook his head as he looked at his watch, it was actually twenty minutes. As he approached the reception desk he noticed the name tag on the young woman standing there. It identified her as "Diane". He quickly introduced himself as he handed her one of his cards.

She shook her head, "I'm sorry, Detective. She's gone."

He was genuinely shocked, "What? You said...."

She nodded and interrupted him "I'm sorry. She was checking out when you called. She overheard me talking to you." She felt bad as she remembered the scene at the desk moments ago. "She said you weren't really a cop. She said you were her ex-boyfriend and were stalking her. She was very convincing. She asked me to lie to you. I didn't see any reason not to believe her."

Clearly, she was genuinely sorry. The pauses and the muffled voices he had heard on the phone now made sense. He was disappointed but he understood. "That's okay, Diane. Thanks anyway. She only has a few minutes on me, did she happen to mention where she was going?"

Diane shook her head, "I'm sorry, she didn't. After I hung up with you I stopped paying attention. I don't know if she left by cab or on foot or what. I'm really sorry."

Sam offered a polite smile as he turned to the exit. The street was a sea of heads walking in all directions. Traffic was moving freely, and there was the steady drone of downtown activity. He replayed in his mind the conversation with John. He was hoping there had been something else in what he had said, something that would have given him a clue as to where she might have gone. He knew she was going to be flying out, but her flight could be in an hour or it could be tomorrow. He thought, “Hell it could days from now. She may have just checked out now but was going to stay with the friends she had mentioned."

He realized that he was starting to panic and knew it was the price for getting emotionally involved in a case. One’s thoughts get clouded, confusion occurs, and then panic takes over. Recognizing the symptoms, he dragged himself back to his usual detached center. He knew how important it was for him to find her - and to find her soon.

21

The uniformed officers were already there as Williams approached the front of the building. The usual perimeter defined by yellow police tape was in place and a small crowd had gathered. He shook his head as he went past, "Vultures" he thought. No matter whether it was a crime scene or a traffic accident, violence always drew a crowd of spectators. He continued inside, donning his surgical gloves as he headed for the apartment with all the activity.

Williams was sure the Lieutenant had assigned this new case as a distraction to get his mind off Sam. It didn't; it only made him angrier thinking of his absence. He decided to use this murder as a showcase of his abilities.

Williams made mental notes of everything he passed on his way through the apartment. There was no sign of a struggle. Everything appeared to be in its place. The forensic technicians were busily doing all their usual chores of crime scene investigation.

When Williams reached the doorway of the bedroom, a photo flash exploded in front of him. He recognized the photographer, "Christ, Mark, did you have to shoot that in my face?"

Mark looked towards the doorway and saw Williams standing there. He laughed, "Sorry, Willie. I didn't see you there." Mark paused, trying to see past Williams, "You flying solo on this one? Where's Yoda?"

Williams looked puzzled, "Yoda?" He thought quickly of The Lucas film, then pictured his partner, "Ah, Davidson. I've never heard that one before. Is that his nickname or something?" He thought it somehow appropriate as Sam probably considered himself the learned one. He laughed when he thought of the character in the movie. "Good one, Mark. I'll have to remember that."

Williams began surveying the scene, "Yoda is out of town following up on some other leads on that Evans thing. He should be back tomorrow or the next day." Williams looked back at Mark, "So, what do we have here?"

Mark shrugged his shoulders and glanced quickly around the room. He replied in a matter-of-fact tone, "It looks like he was just sitting here beside the computer. He was facing the bed. A single gun shot wound in the forehead - three-fifty-seven by the looks of the entry wound. There is no sign of a struggle so pretty safe to assume he knew the shooter."

Williams nodded his head. His voice had no discernible emotion, "Yeah. Well let's have a look." He walked the rest of the way into the room and towards the male body in the chair. The entry wound was above the level of his eyebrows and almost precisely in the middle of his eyes. "Nice shot. Facial surgery by artillery." He chuckled quietly to himself, and thought of how neatly bullets shatter a skull and push the eyes apart. Everything looks to be intact, and if it wasn't for the small hole in the forehead one wouldn't know anything was amiss. The back of the head showed all the damage. The victim's blood, pieces of flesh, and fragments of bone covered the whole area behind him. Williams looked back at Mark and chuckled, "So what makes you think he was facing the bed."

Mark laughed, "Gee, I don't know. You're the detective. You tell me."

Williams' attention went back to the debris field. He noticed the area of the heaviest concentration on the wall, and in the center - a hole.

Mark's eyes followed Williams' line of vision. "They found the slug on the floor back there. It was pretty messed up. Don't think ballistics will get anything there."

Williams looked back at Mark and nodded his head. "No doubt, that slug saw a fair amount of activity during its flight." His attention returned to the man in the chair. He squatted slightly, looking at the entry wound on the forehead, then to the hole in the wall. He pictured in his mind the flight path of the bullet and tried to see where the death ship had started its voyage. It was clearly pointing toward the bottom edge of the bed, almost exactly in the middle. He thought out loud, "Shooter was sitting on the edge of the bed. Gun raised and fired."

He looked at Mark, and pointed to the bed, "Mark, sit there and point at him, will ya."

Mark held his fingers up like they were a gun and pointed towards the victim. Williams moved Mark's arm through several positions, trying to duplicate the angle, but couldn't. "You're too tall. How tall are you?"

Mark smiled, "5 foot 11."

Williams smiled "Okay, shooter is probably 5 foot 2 to 5 foot 5. No more than that." Williams' eyes wandered to the victim's lap. That's when he noticed the man's crotch. His pants were down slightly and wide open. His eyes didn't move, "Mark. Get them in here. I want a swab of his dick."

Mark was a little surprised by that, "What the hell?"

Williams chuckled and turned to Mark, "I'll bet our shooter was a woman. He didn't just know her, they were probably very close." He pointed back to the victim. "It doesn't look like he made any attempt to get out of the chair. I don't know about you, but if someone pointed a gun in my face I think I would be inclined to try and get the hell out of the way. The poor bastard was probably totally oblivious to what was about to happen."

Mark got off the bed and headed out of the room. He paused at the door and looked back at Williams, "Davidson had better start watching his back. We're gonna start calling you Yoda if you're not careful."

Williams looked back at him and smiled, "Don't you dare. Willie is good enough. I'm still a prick."

As Williams continued to survey the scene, the computer caught his attention. There had to be some significance to it. He was on a roll and wished Davidson was here to watch him work. The monitor was off but the light on the computer tower indicated it was still under power. He reached for his pencil and pushed in the switch. There was a faint hiss as the screen came to life.

Mark was back with a technician, and Williams turned to them as they entered the room. He saw the look on the technicians face. He knew what was going through his mind, "Just do it, all right. We're looking for, lipstick, saliva, semen - like that."

The technician's expression turned professional and he reached for the victim's pants. Williams turned back to the computer, "Ok, let's see what we have here."

The screen displayed a long list of records. It took him a few seconds, but Williams soon realized they were the records of a sperm bank. A few seconds later Williams found the clinic's name. He was surprised and quickly turned back to Mark. "Anyone got a name on our losing contestant here."

Mark replied without hesitation, "Yeah, it's Smythe.... Dwayne Smythe."

Williams recognized the name from the Evans' case. He looked back to the man in the chair, "Do we have a time of death?"

The forensic technician answered that question without looking up from his task. Williams realized the implications immediately, and he now believed that this murder was related to the death of Philip. The same caliber of weapon was used and the sperm bank connection to Angela. He believed it was the same shooter in both cases. The time frame worked, and the coincidences were too great. He also realized that Angela and Elaine were at the station with him at the time of this shooting. "Damn" he thought. "Davidson was right." Angela and Elaine were innocent, and now he would have to admit to his partner that he had been wrong. He muttered under his breath again, "Damn."

The forensic technician looked up from his work "Hey, Willie, did you notice this?"

Williams looked down at him, "Notice what?"

The technician smiled realizing Williams had missed it. "Perfume. There's a distinct smell of perfume on the pant legs around his thighs." He paused to let that sink in. "Pretty good guess that someone had their head between his legs. Smells like..." He recognized the fragrance and searched his memory for the name. "That's it. It's Charlie."

* * * * *

Elaine stood at the door of the bedroom looking through its partial opening. Her daughter was asleep on top of the linens. Elaine smiled thinking how peaceful she looked. For a moment everything that had been going on didn't exist. Her baby was in her bed safe from the world.

She realized it was only a delusion and that her daughter was simply exhausted. The trauma of the day had taken its toll. Elaine quietly closed the door and headed back downstairs. In the living room, Dave and Simon were standing by the bar chatting. Elaine was grateful they had stayed.

Elaine wished it all would just go away so their lives could get back to normal. However, she knew that would never happen. Nothing would ever be the same again. Her daughter's view of the world was now forever changed.

Elaine sat on the couch and looked into the still lit fireplace and watched the flames dancing on the logs. She could hear the faint murmur of conversation outside the house as her mind wandered back to Angela's youth. She pictured Angela laughing and playing in the yard. She could see her smiles at her various parties. She visualized her eyes so big and bright as they sat in this very room talking late into the night. She began to cry openly. The tears flowed freely following the channels time had cut in her face.

All the men could do was stand by and watch helplessly. There was nothing they could do to change the facts. They hoped their presence, at least, brought some measure of comfort.

* * * * *

Sam was making progress. He had cleared his mind and was acting like the detective he preferred to be. All the airlines had been very cooperative, and in time, he was able to find the one Lisa booked. Relieved, he discovered her flight wasn't leaving until the next morning. It would be the 7:15 a.m. to Mexico City. He would be at the airport long before check in time and he would wait.

He called the Lieutenant and brought him up to date on his progress. Surprisingly, the Lieutenant had displayed some excitement. He had said he wouldn't be satisfied until Lisa was back, booked, and spilling her guts. That was enough for Sam to know he was excited.

The Lieutenant promised to fax a photo of Lisa to the hotel before morning. Sam thought it would probably be only an enlargement of her driver's license but that would be good enough. He made arrangements with his hotel for one more night and then went for supper. After he ate, he decided to let John know it was almost over. It was a police matter and these facts really didn't concern John. Still, he felt a need to do it.

He returned to the hotel to freshen up. He stopped at the reception desk to see if the fax had arrived. The young man at the desk retrieved several sheets and handed them to Sam.

As he headed for the elevator Sam glanced at the image on the first sheet. The face he saw surprised him - he recognized it. He was sure he had seen her somewhere before, but couldn't remember where. It was recently, but where, he had no idea.

He threw the papers on his bed and went to freshen up. When he returned, he started to read the other pages that came with the photo. It was Lisa's lengthy police file. She had been in and out of trouble for most of her life - mostly small stuff. When he returned to the photo, it hit him again. Where had he seen her? He cursed his memory, and headed for his rental car.

Driving to John's house his mind was totally preoccupied with the photo. In a flash, he suddenly remembered how he knew Lisa. He pushed the accelerator pedal to the floor, hoping he wasn't too late. He slammed an open hand into the steering wheel as he drove, "Damn, Damn."

It had been his subconscious working that had made him so interested in going back to see John. He had thought it was an urge to share his success with him, but now he knew it was to warn him. John was in mortal danger.

Arriving at the house he wasted no time getting to the front door. He was about to knock when he saw the door ajar. He mumbled to himself, "Shit!" and drew his gun from its holster. He took a deep breath as he squatted to the side of the door. He used the barrel to push the door full open. As the door ceased its travel he thought he should wait and call for back up. Going in alone could be extremely dangerous. He carefully looked around the doorjamb and quickly returned to his position at its side.

He took a moment to process everything his eyes had captured in that brief instant. He had seen the two bodies in the living room, motionless. No one else had been visible. He took another deep breath and proceeded through the door, still in the squatted position.

Once inside, with his back against the wall, he looked into the living room again. He recognized the two bodies he had seen. It was John and his sister. Even from this distance it was obvious they were dead. He was annoyed for not having arrived sooner. "Damn!"

The smell of burnt gunpowder was still fresh in the air. He could hear noises coming from the kitchen. He didn't move as he identified the sounds. They were the sounds of food cooking and water boiling over a pot. He also detected the faint scent of a woman's perfume and recognized it as "Charlie".

He continued to scan the scene, smell the air, and listened for any other sounds. He was satisfied that the three of them were the only ones in the house. He stood up and proceeded to the living room, holstering his weapon.

He put his finger to the neck of each, doubting he would detect a pulse. He muttered again, "Damn." Hovering over Jill, he leaned forward and smelled her neck. Although almost overpowered by the distinct aroma of the blood in which she was lying, he detected the fragrance of bath soap and nodded. She wasn't wearing "Charlie".

He reached for the phone on the side table and called 911. He identified himself to the operator and quickly made a report. When he hung up, he started scrutinizing the scene further. He knew in a couple of minutes the place would be full of the local police. If there was any information here, he would have to find it quickly.

He reviewed the lay of the room, the position of the bodies, and tried to imagine what had happened during those critical few seconds. There were no clear signs any struggles. No signs, he thought, except for the two bodies. Jill was lying on the floor, face down. She had three distinct entry wounds in her back and her head was pointed out of the living room.

John was lying sideways on the couch; a single entry wound in the center of his forehead and he was facing into the living room. Almost directly in front of the couch, on the opposite side of the room was a fireplace, in which a fire still burned. Beside it, to the left of Jill's body, and a few feet behind her, was an armchair. On the opposite side of the room was a love seat. In the center of the room, framed by those three pieces of furniture was a coffee table. Sam proceeded to the love seat. He looked back at the two bodies to see how their final positions related to this position. The angles were wrong.

He moved slowly sideways and with every subtle movement he checked his position against the position of the two bodies. Finally, he was satisfied he had found the right one. He thought out loud, "Ok, she was standing here." He formed his hand into a pretend gun and pointed towards the couch. Slowly he moved his hand until it pointed to the place where Jill was shot.

He examined the areas behind the bodies where material had been sprayed by the exit of the slugs. He now had a pretty good idea what had happened. He went over the whole scene in his mind, reconstructing the events.

"John was sitting there." He pointed at the couch were John still was, "Jill would have been sitting there." He pointed to the armchair, then paused and nodded. "No doubt, that's right. Shooter was standing here." He looked to the position he was standing in. "She pulled her gun. It must have happened pretty quickly. John must have been distracted, or totally in shock. She didn't hesitate. Bang! One shot right between the eyes!"

He looked at his position again, and then over to where John would have been sitting, "Damn good shot. Or lucky." and he shook his head. "Jill would have seen it happen and stood to run out of the room. Shooter spun to her and bang! Down she went."

He looked at her remains lying on the floor again and shook his head remorsefully and then looked to the exit debris, "There isn't enough." He looked back at her body again and was suddenly disgusted, "Damn cold bitch. Jill would have had been hit once and then fell to the floor. Shooter would have watched it happen, waited until she hit the floor and then popped her two more times." He shook his head again at the thought of it. He was sure when the locals arrived and moved the body they would find two slugs in the floor beneath her.

The sound of the approaching sirens broke his concentration. It didn't matter, he had figured out the events as they had occurred and was sure the culprit was Lisa. He reached into his jacket pocket, pulled out his badge and clipped it to the front of his sports coat. Then he pulled out his notepad and started making notes.

He heard the first car screech to a halt in front of the house, then a second, then a third, and then a fourth. A young uniform came bursting through the front door, his weapon drawn. He caught a glimpse of Sam and spun, pointing his weapon at him.

Sam looked up him and smiled, "I would really prefer you didn't shoot."

The officer noticed his badge, and holstered his weapon, "Detective? Sorry. What have you got?"

Sam looked over the scene again and then looked back at the officer, "I don't know about you, but I'd call it a violent crime." and he chuckled to himself.

The officer was not amused, "No shit, Detective."

Another man came in dressed in a style similar to Sam, "Davidson, I take it?"

Sam smiled and kept making his notes.

"I'm Detective Henry. Things a little quiet back home, thought you'd go on the road?" His tone was distinctly sarcastic.

It made Sam stop writing and look up. He suddenly liked this detective and actually wanted to share his story with him. "I'm here following up on some leads from a case back home - the Evans' murder. I think we have the same shooter here."

Henry's eyebrows rose, "Oh yeah, Evans. I saw something about that on the tube. His new wife popped him or something. Nothing like true love." He chuckled.

Sam realized the press was still passing along the wrong information - probably spicier than the truth. He was suddenly annoyed, "No. She definitely had nothing to do with it. I'm looking for an ex-employee of Mr. Evans - one Lisa Douglas. I believe she is responsible for his death, and for the murder of these two."

Henry waved Sam out of the living room and pointed to the front door, smiling "Let's you and me have us a little chat outside." Sam nodded and headed towards the front door. A small group of men were coming in as they exited. He recognized their equipment as that of the forensic team. He wanted to see their full report as soon as it was ready. He would mention that to Henry.

As he passed through the front door he thought of Mr. Malcolm. "Shit, Jill's husband. Hey Henry, her husband doesn't know yet."

Henry shrugged his shoulders, "He will soon enough. Come on, let's sit in my car. I want to hear everything."

The sun was down and the lights from the police vehicles bathed the immediate area with a glow of red and blue. The small crowd that gathered were illuminated by the lights.

As they settled themselves in Henry's car, the thought crossed Sam's mind that Lisa would not be taking her morning flight. Sam started, "Henry, I think we have a problem. This Lisa bitch is supposed to be catching a flight in the morning. She heard me talking to

Diane at the hotel. I think that's why we're all here having this party. She came over to thank John and Jill in person for assisting me. I'm sure she has changed her plans and is looking for a new way out. We have to find her."

Henry looked confused, "Hold up there stranger. Just what the hell are you talking about?"

Sam smiled realizing this officer had no idea what all had happened. The whole investigation was beyond Henry's knowledge. He chuckled to himself for his brief moment of stupidity. "Sorry Henry, of course you don't know. I arrived……"

22

Sam pulled into the closest available parking spot. It was raining hard and the sky was black. The weather matched his mood. Even though he expected Lisa to abandon her one way, nonrefundable, first class ticket to Mexico, he had to be here.

She hadn't booked any other flights on any of the other airlines - at least not in her own name, and Sam was sure she hadn't had enough time to acquire fake identification. Still he was here, just in case. Besides, there are many other ways to leave the country. That is, if she were planning on leaving at all.

As he entered the terminal, he could see the myriad of people busily rushing about. Some were standing in long lines looking depressed, while others were sitting in the lounge areas in resigned patience. He smiled a knowing pity for them all.

A young boy went running by giggling, obviously unconcerned about location or atmosphere, bent only on amusing himself. His mother was in close pursuit looking decidedly stressed. Sam thought how much easier life would be if we could retain that child's perspective - too young to know stress, real fear, or real pain, enjoying every second of the day without a significant care in the world.

Sam shook his head again "I have got to stay away from airports. They really screw with my head," and he chuckled to himself at that.

Sam quickly found an empty chair overlooking the check-in counters. If Lisa did arrive, he would be able to spot her. All the airlines had been alerted to watch for her. If she tried to get on a flight they were to detain her, and notify the police.

As he sat waiting, Sam thought of the host of other possible scenarios. Maybe Lisa never intended to fly at all. Perhaps she simply purchased the ticket as a diversion should the need arise. She could have acquired forged documents in the past and booked a flight under an assumed name, purchasing the ticket with her real name to throw him off the scent.

He shook his head. Lisa's possible movements were wild guesses at best. He simply didn't have enough information on her to build a profile. His mind wandered to yesterday's conversation with Henry. He had been quick to offer his assistance and support, for which Sam was very grateful. As a result, the task of getting Lisa's image out to every enforcement and ticket agency had been almost easy and certainly quicker than if he had done it himself. A net had been placed over the entire country.

However, the problem with nets is the open spaces. If one uses the right net, the catch is assured, a wrong net and the quarry swims right through - sometimes unaware the net was there at all.

Sam shook off that thought, he needed to stay positive. He was sure they were going to catch Lisa - she would pay for her crimes! "Revenge!" The thought passed quickly through his mind.

The flight time came and went. She hadn't come. He was disappointed but not surprised. He approached the check-in counter, produced his badge, identified himself, and asked for a check of the passenger manifest. He needed to be sure he hadn't missed her. Before long the ticket agent confirmed that she hadn't arrived and no one matching her description had boarded the plane.

He smiled politely, thanked them for their efforts, and left the terminal. He had exhausted all his leads. The locals were now fully aware of the connection between the deaths of John and Jill, and Evans, and he trusted that they would be giving this case their full attention.

Sam brought the car to life and headed back to his hotel to check out. He would return home and check Williams' progress. He felt bad as he suddenly realized he hadn't talked to his partner since he left. He had spoken to the Lieutenant a couple of times but not his partner. He knew just how annoyed he would be if his partner had left him out of the loop. He would apologize to Williams when he got back. He didn't hate Williams, he was new is all, and didn't know Sam's ways. Sam decided that he would take him out for a beer and try to get to know him better.

* * * * *

Sam walked into the squad room and searched for Williams. Phil was sitting at the first desk Sam passed and looked up, "Hey, Yoda. How goes the battle?" he laughed loudly.

"Screw you, Phil," and thought immediately of Mark. Sam liked what the comparison was meant to signify, he just hated hearing that name. "I was wondering how long it would take Mark to spread that one. You had better be careful Phil or I'll call your wife and tell her what you were really doing on that stake out."

Sam knew Phil was a loyal husband and he would never do anything to hurt his wife. The threat was hollow - simple retaliation for his comment. Phil knew it, and was still smiling, "Oh Yoda, take a pill or something. Besides, it wasn't Mark. It was your buddy, wee Willie."

"Willie? How the hell..." Sam was surprised he knew the handle. "Where is he anyway? I need my hello kiss."

Phil smiled, blew Sam a kiss, and chuckled, "I think he's in with the Lieutenant?" With that Phil went back to perusing the papers that covered his desk.

Sam looked towards the Lieutenant's office and then back at Phil. "Thanks Phil. Don't forget, you still owe me a beer. The Lions' lost." Sam chuckled quietly as he headed towards the Lieutenant's office. Phil uttered a soft grunt.

Reaching the office door, Sam gave it a quick rap and proceeded through. The conversation between Williams and the Lieutenant ended abruptly. The Lieutenant looked up at him, "Christ, Sam! At least you knocked this time." He was only half joking.

Sam smiled at him, "Fine, thank you. Yes, very productive. I'm happy to see you too."

The Lieutenant didn't smile, "Sit down and shut up."

Sam chuckled quietly as he complied, "So what's been going on since I left. Everything grind to a halt did it?"

"That's right, Sam. You go away, and we all sit around pining until you get back." The Lieutenant closed the file on his desk and tossed it towards him, "Here read this or should I have Mr. Williams read it to you?"

Sam reached for the file and suddenly a surprised look crossed his face. "Mr. Williams?" He looked shocked at his partner. That was the first time he had heard the Lieutenant refer to him by his name. "Okay, what the hell is going on?"

Williams wore a broad smile and pointed to the file in Sam's hand, "Just read, Yoda. Read and learn."

Sam's eyebrows rose as he opened the file and started to read. It was the Smythe murder investigation report. As he read, he made a variety of responsive sounds - all indicating his approval of its contents.

When he had finished, he closed the file and tossed it onto the Lieutenant's desk. He looked towards Williams and smiled, "Nice piece of work. It certainly supports my theories. Let me tell you about my little jaunt."

Sam proceeded to brief them on everything that had happened. He was feeling a new respect for his partner and as a result, conveyed his information without his usual colour.

There were still a few things about the case that bothered Williams and with this new congenial atmosphere in the office, he felt comfortable bringing them up. "What about the note? This Lisa chick obviously drenched herself in that perfume. Any traces of it on the note? Can we tie it to her?"

Sam looked stunned and stared at the Lieutenant, "You didn't tell him?"

Williams was curious, "Tell him? Tell me what?" His eyes darted back and forth between the Lieutenant and Sam.

The Lieutenant was annoyed, "I was about to when you came barging in. I think you should tell him. By the way, it was Lopez."

It was Sam's turn to be surprised, "Lopez? Ha! I would never have guessed him."

Williams was getting annoyed. These two obviously had a secret they weren't sharing with him. "What the hell is going on?"

Sam saw this as an opportunity to have some fun with his partner but remembered his vow. He gathered up his thoughts and then proceeded. "There was never any doubt as to whether Evan's death was a murder - no note and no gun! That's why we got the call in the first place." He paused there for a second, reflecting.

"There's been a leak in the department and privileged information was finding its way to the media. We saw this as a perfect chance to ferret out the culprit." He paused again. He just couldn't let this opportunity go.

"Didn't you think it was a little odd that we didn't find a weapon at the scene? Weren't you a little suspicious when we went to interview Mrs. Evans under the premise of suicide and then the first headline of the day was 'foul play suspected'" He paused again.

Williams expressions changed from surprise, to curiosity, and then to anger. He had noticed there hadn't been a gun. He had simply assumed Sam had already taken it, bagged, tagged, and processed it without telling him, and had done the same with the note. He had just assumed Sam was so used to working alone that he had simply ignored him. "You didn't think I should have known about this."

Williams' mind returned to the memory of the second time they had gone to see Angela. Williams almost screamed, "We went back there to arrest her. Momma dear starts spilling her guts, and you just sat there. You knew all along."

The Lieutenant looked at him, "Yeah, we should have told you but the leak started about the time you transferred in. You weren't above suspicion. It was my call. Get over it. Sam, continue."

Sam looked at his partner and almost felt sorry for him. "I think that's enough about that. He was murdered, point blank between the eyes." He looked back at the Lieutenant, "Ballistics?"

The Lieutenant smiled, "Yep, same gun in all cases. She's the one. I think we're certain of it now. All we have to do is find her."

Angela and Elaine suddenly came to Sam's mind, "Lieutenant, you are going to release a statement? We have to clear Angela's name in this."

The Lieutenant looked pained. It was the first time Sam had seen the Lieutenant looking as though he regretted a decision. He nodded in response to the question, "Yeah, I'll take care of that." He paused, "I'm going to need your report on Simmons and his sister ASAP."

Sam nodded, "Yeah, no problem, first thing in the morning. I got some things I need to do, okay?"

The Lieutenant nodded and began looking over the stacks of files on his desk. Sam took that as a cue to leave. As he got up, Williams spoke. His voice was strong and forceful, "I want a transfer."

"No!" was the Lieutenant's immediate response. He didn't even look up.

Williams was equally quick responding to that, "Yes! I want out of here. I can't work like this. I'm a damn good detective, I deserve better than this."

The Lieutenant looked up and folded his hands on his desk, "Look, I'm sorry about all this. I had my reasons. It wasn't anything personal. You are a good detective. You and Sam are going to make a good team, I'm sure of it." Realizing he was approaching sensitive, he quickly shook it off. "But, know this. I'm not your mother. You got a problem then take it up with your partner. This is the last time I am going to hold you to my breast and pat you on the head. Grow up and deal with it. Now get your ass out of my office."

Williams smiled feeling somewhat better. He realized for the first time what the Lieutenant was about. He liked the idea of a commanding officer that cared about his people. He still thought he was as a jerk, but he could identify with that.

As Williams passed Sam, he smacked him hard on the shoulder, "Okay, Yoda. Let's us do some detecting." and he laughed.

Sam winced at the pain and looked at the Lieutenant. His head was back down reading, but Sam was sure he caught a glimpse of him smiling. It made him smile himself and he shook his head. He followed Williams out of the office and closed the door behind him.

No sooner was the door closed when he realized that he had forgotten the Smythe file. He turned and walked through the door without knocking. The Lieutenant was still sitting with his head down. The file Sam wanted was in the Lieutenant's hand, held out to the approaching detective. Sam walked to the desk and took it from him. There was sincerity in his voice, "Thanks, Lieutenant."

The lieutenant knew what he meant - it wasn't about the file "You're welcome. Now piss off, I have work to do." Davidson smiled and left.

23

Sam arrived at Elaine's just after six. He needed to tidy up some loose ends and in order to do that he needed some more answers from Angela. He could have waited until another time, but for personal reasons, it had to be now.

The Lieutenant had given the statement to the media, and solicited their help in publicizing the image of Lisa. Sam knew that before long virtually everyone in the country would have seen a picture of Lisa. He was confident there was no place she could hide. It was just a matter of time before she was found.

* * * * *

Lisa's car moved through the street, guided only by her instincts. Slowing, stopping, accelerating, and avoidance were handled by her subconscious; her conscious mind was only marginally aware of the car's path through town. The images of her life played over again and again in her mind. Everything she had known, everything she had done, flashed past her as if displayed on a movie screen.

Only selected images lingered long enough for her to recognize and process. There was her early childhood. It was a warm summer day and she and her parents were at the beach. The sun was shining, the waves were crashing ashore, and the gulls circled overhead singing their songs.

They ran, played games, and laughed. The whole day was a pleasure. It was the pure joy experienced by loving families sharing time together. Then her memory grew black. Night had come and she was sleeping in her bed. A familiar sound woke her. It was her father. He was in her room and it was very late.

After that, the memory dimmed. The horror was more than her mind was prepared to recall. It was the first time he had come to her in the night but it wasn't the last. She had loved him so very much, but that night her love ended and the hate began. Her mother did nothing, yet she surely must have known, but he kept coming.

* * * * *

As Sam came around the corner he could see Elaine's house. The crowds were all but gone but those that remained approached him with questions. They wanted him to comment on the new evidence. How could they be so sure Angela was innocent? Who was Lisa Douglas? What was the connection between Lisa and Mr. and Mrs. Evans? What were the police going to do to make up for the accusations they had made against Mrs. Evans?

Although he would have liked to comment, it wasn't his job. The force had experts to handle those matters. All he wanted now was to talk to Angela. These last few reporters would soon be gone and then Angela and Elaine would be able to get on with their lives.

* * * * *

Lisa's memories paused again at her adolescence. She was thirteen or fourteen when she met him. He was eighteen, an older man. Under his tutelage she became involved with drugs, shoplifting, and even prostitution. The horror that was now her life made it easy for her to follow him. He taught her how to ride and shoot, and he was the one thing in life she loved. However, her encounters with the police were becoming increasingly frequent.

Her mind reeled again and stopped on a day at the shooting range. This day was different. She didn't remember all the details, but the sight of him lying dead in a pool of his own blood was etched into her mind. The police said it had been an accident, but since that day, the image of him lying there was often on her mind, and frequently disturbed her sleep. Even after all these years she still didn't believe it was an accident.

* * * * *

Saunders answered the door and escorted Sam into the living room. The room was dark, lit only by the light from the foyer. Sam promptly took position in front of the fireplace.

Saunders and Smith maintained their vigil by the front door, providing a barrier between that space and this. With faces void of expression, they looked as intimidating as ever. Simon and Dave stood by the bar and looked back at Sam. They too appeared emotionless. They stood quietly, waiting to see what had brought Sam there.

Elaine and Angela were sitting on the couch holding hands; Janet was beside them. Looking into Angela's sad eyes, Sam thought how old they now made her appear. He looked away disgusted.

The wedding picture on the mantle caught his eye, and he looked at it for a few seconds. It was a nice shot of the bride and groom with Elaine and Simon standing just behind the newlyweds. The four were flanked by the bridesmaids and groomsmen. They all looked so happy then. Looking at the faces now in front of him, the contrast was startling.

Something was amiss in the room. Sam initially thought it was their displeasure with him but now he thought it was something else. It suddenly occurred to him that they didn't know. He frowned and looked directly at Elaine. "Haven't you been listening to the news?"

Her expression didn't change, "News? You have got to be kidding. Why would we be watching the news?"

With what they have had been through, he thought, "Why indeed?" He knew that he was going to be the bearer of good news and it made him smile. Looking at Angela he thought of Simmons. That bit of news was going to be hard and his warm feeling was extinguished.

Without knowing what had happened, they would probably find the questions he was about to ask very strange. Still, Angela had the information he needed to complete his profile of Lisa and he wanted it.

* * * * *

Lisa's mind reeled again and stopped at another point some weeks later. She was staying at a friend's house and under the dark blanket of night she stole away to her parent's house. There in the dark she could see her parents asleep in their bed. They looked so peaceful.

The next morning the police arrived at her girlfriend's house. They woke her to inform her of the robbery that had gone bad. She had not even been a suspect, and ever since then the thought of that night brought a smile to her face. She had hoped that if she did what the voices told her, they would stop. She was wrong.

The voices continued and she finally accepted them as a part of herself and always followed their orders.

After that night she went to live with her aunt and uncle and things were better. The voices still came but their orders were different. She began to act and appear as any other teen. Soon her history became common knowledge but the specifics remained a guarded secret.

* * * * *

Sam, surprised they hadn't heard the news, decided to get the information he needed before he told them. Then he would delicately tell her about Simmons. He wasn't looking forward to that.

He picked up the picture from the mantle and pointing to it, he asked, "Angela. What can you tell me about Lisa Douglas?" His voice was calm and professional.

Her eyebrows rose slightly. It looked for a moment, as if she may display emotion but that was as far as she would commit herself. Her face remained cold, "Lisa? What about her?" Her gaze wandered to the picture.

It had been this picture with Lisa's image that Sam had remembered. Sam felt sorry for Angela, and could only imagine the difficult time they had had over the last several days. Now he recognized what it was he saw in her – it was innocence lost! Her face told the story of just how bad things had been and he hoped, when it was finally over, she would be able to put it behind her.

* * * * *

Then Lisa thought of Philip. He was an incredible man - an icon in her mind. She was determined to make him hers. She got close to him at every opportunity and she could not understand why he never responded to her.

Then there was Angela. Her good friend, Angela, who stole Philip away from her knowing full well he was hers. Angela ignored Lisa when she confronted her about Philip. The voices began talking to Lisa again.

When Angela announced their engagement, Lisa knew what she must do. Lisa had grown into an attractive, intelligent woman, who had learned patience. What had to be done would be done, in due course. She would bide her time, get close to them, be trusted by them and when the time was right, she would do what needed to be done.

Angela and Philip continued on their course, and Lisa remained close. She was there through the engagement and wedding, always supportive and helpful. The rage inside her continued to grow, undetected. During the dark, lonely nights the voices would come, and together they conspired and developed their plan.

* * * * *

Sam forced himself back to the present, "Yeah, Lisa Douglas. Tell me what you know about her. How did you meet her?"

Angela looked at him for a few seconds trying to figure out what he was up to. Clearly, he was trying to accomplish something but she couldn't discern what and decided that she really didn't care. She remembered her high school days, her old classmates, and all the good times she had back then.

"Lisa was a classmate of mine. We went to high school together. She had been in trouble a few times, nothing serious. She is one of my best friends." She paused for a moment, "Actually, it was because of her that I met Philip."

Sam wasn't sure why but when she said those words he felt shock. He controlled himself and spoke, "Okay, you were friends. Tell me more about her and Philip."

That phrase caught Angela off guard. "Lisa and Philip?" Sam nodded his head. After a few moments, Angela continued. "In school, we all had part time jobs. Lisa worked for Philip's company after school and on weekends. He was only starting out in those days. The business was nothing like it is now." Pausing again, she allowed a small smile to creep across her face, "She had a bit of a crush on him but he didn't know she existed. We used to joke that she was going to marry him someday. She used to get so mad at us." Thinking of it made her smile vanish.

"Anyway, even in those days, Philip was always trying to play the nice guy. He used to throw parties for his employees. Lisa always invited us and we always went. They were usually fun." She paused again remembering those events.

"It was at one of those parties that I met Philip. It was a year or so ago." It surprised her that she didn't remember the exact date. It was one of the most significant nights in her life and the memory of it was incomplete.

She pointed to the picture in Sam's hand. "We always hung out together at these parties but one night

Philip asked me to dance. He always worked the room and danced with all the women as if it was his duty. But that night was different, one thing led to another and we started going out." She paused. "I remember Lisa had been so mad at me. She accused me of stealing her boyfriend. We had a really nasty fight, but that was it. After that we were still good friends. I think she understood how silly the whole thing had been. He hadn't been interested in her. I don't think he would even recognize her if they were standing face to face somewhere. He was only interested in me. When we got engaged, she was very happy for us. She wanted so badly to be in the wedding party." She thought of her wedding but instead of smiling, she shuddered.

"She still works for his company. Actually, I think she's away on business right now. She goes on a fair number of business trips for the company. She's on the sales team." Angela paused again, searching her memory. She was satisfied she had relayed all the relevant information. "There you have it. That's the whole story. So what of it? Your turn? What's the big deal about Lisa?"

Sam now understood the connection, and how things had unfolded. He felt pity for Angela. She was innocent in this but was the one suffering the most. "Life can be so unfair," he thought.

Sam wanted to tell her the good news, hoping it would somehow make things better. "You've been exonerated in this whole matter." He paused to let that sink in.

Angela focused on his face, as did her mother. Angela kept herself under control, "Excuse me?"

"I've been following your... I've been away following up on some leads. We now know for certain that you are innocent in this. We have set up a nation wide search for Lisa."

Angela heard the words but it took a few seconds for their meaning to sink in. "My God. Lisa? She did this?" There was no mistaking the horror in her voice. "We had lunch just a few days ago. Actually, it was a couple of days before Philip's last trip." She shook her head again in disbelief. "She wanted to hear all about the honeymoon. We met for lunch. She seemed so happy for us. We talked about everything. I told her about my father; his name; what he was doing; how difficult it had been to find him. I told her about Philip's upcoming business trip, where he was going, and were he'd be staying. I had no idea."

These new pieces of information made Sam shiver. He had been doing this job a long time and thought he had seen and heard it all. He imagined what must have been going through Lisa's mind. It amazed him just how cold and calculating some people can be.

* * * * *

Lisa's memory skipped and then stopped on the night that Philip had come back to her room. She was sure he had recognized her, maybe he hadn't. It didn't matter really. She had been able to convince him with little resistance. The camera was just part of the fun. He was such a stupid man. How could he not know what the pictures would be used for? Maybe he did, and simply didn't care.

Lisa's memory skipped on to Dwayne. He was such a brilliant man, so caring and naive. It had simply been a night for fun - a little recreational physical pleasure. When she went to his apartment and saw the computers and heard his story, she knew it would be much more.

She had shared her plans for Philip and Angela with Dwayne but he wanted no part of it and even said he would call the police. She couldn't allow that to happen. They had already made a great deal of money and she wouldn't allow him to destroy that. She would have her share and his, but not until she had taken care of Philip. Dwayne couldn't know about that, though. She had convinced him she was only joking. He was such a love struck fool she could convince him of anything.

* * * * *

Sam placed the photograph carefully on the mantle and cleared his throat. There was compassion in his voice. "Thank you, Angela. That was the final piece I was missing."

He stood silently, ordering his thoughts. He looked at Angela and knew he could tell her only the facts, not his beliefs nor Lisa's true motivations. He knew how they would affect her and he wouldn't do that.

"As far as I can determine, Lisa set Philip up for blackmail. As you said, Lisa worked for Philip on the sales team. She knew he would be going on that trip, and where he'd be staying."

He hoped saying that would prevent her from thinking that somehow it had been her fault. "She had a camera in the room. She was obviously confident she could get him back there. She may even have drugged him. We don't know any of that for certain." He didn't believe that for one second, feeling sure Philip was a willing participant.

"On the day Philip was killed, as best as we can determine, she contacted him and set up a meeting in his office. She probably showed him the photos and demanded money. We do know he made out a check to her. We don't know why they met again later that night. That's all speculation. Maybe he had originally turned her down, and later decided to pay. We just don't know. But they did meet at the beach and she killed him." He knew he was being blunt but there was no point to sugar coating.

When he thought of the media he realized they would also have the story of Smythe. The connection would be made and reported. "Better get it all out now," he thought.

"She was dating Dwayne Smythe, you know? She killed him, too." He looked into Angela's eyes to see if there was any reaction. There wasn't. "We think we know when they started going together. He had made a deposit of a large sum of money in his bank. We found receipts from a number of shops, dated the same day. We also found a matchbook cover from a local night club with Lisa's name and phone number on it. We think he went out that night on the prowl, met her, and they started seeing each other." He hated the thought of going into too much detail.

"We also found that over time he had made several other deposits of fifty thousand dollars each and believe they were from other people like you. We think Lisa was also involved in that enterprise or at least she knew about it. The day Smythe was killed all the money in that account was transferred out. We think she killed him for the money."

Angela was openly shocked. She couldn't believe that she had been that close to Lisa and really didn't know her. She couldn't believe that Lisa had been able to so completely take her in with the good, supportive friend act. Angela shivered at the thought of it. Suddenly she thought of her father, "My God, my father. She knew about my father. Not just what I told her, but everything. Dwayne had all that information."

A thought quickly flashed across Sam's mind, "Simmons was Angela's father. How many others had he fathered? It was possible there could be dozens." He shook it off. He couldn't think about that right now.

* * * * *

Lisa's memories were no longer sequential. The chronological order blurred but the events themselves were still vivid. She recalled that day with Philip in his office. She convinced him to meet with her. She demanded money or she would expose him to Angela. In her mind, she would get the money then she would kill him. These were all things that were necessary. He had been quick to give her the check, almost eager. She left most of the pictures with him, but not all. She wanted some mementos for herself. Besides, he would never know. It really didn't matter if he knew or not, his life was over, he just wasn't aware of it yet.

Later that day she had been able to convince him to meet her again at the beach. She told him that she was sorry and wanted to give back the money. He was such a fool, he actually came. The gun felt comfortable in her hand, it always did. It was like an extension of her body.

The deed done, she returned to Dwayne. Soon everything in her life would be good again. She needed to share the joy of her accomplishment. Dwayne was sitting in his usual place at the computer. She entered the room, disrobed, and did things to him that made him feel as good as she felt. Soon he would feel nothing at all.

He was sitting back in his chair glowing when she told him what she had done. The gun, her only real friend, the only thing that ever truly helped her, was in her hand and she stared him in the eye. He heard the words, saw the gun, and realized the inevitable. There was no reaction from him at all. He gazed upon her beautiful naked body waiting for what he knew she must do. He didn't have to wait long. In that brief instant, he felt remorse for all that happened and prayed quietly for forgiveness.

She looked upon his lifeless body and thought how proud she was of him. He knew what was going to happen and he took it like a man. She looked at the computer screen and saw what he had been doing before she had come. It was a file she had found herself, days before. It was the file that brought all the truths to her. Angela's real father and her real father, not the animal she had grown up with, were the same man. They were more than friends, they were sisters.

Lisa hated Angela even more. She remembered the joy Angela had felt at having found her father and how they had grown so close. It was just one more thing that Lisa couldn't allow, one more thing that Angela had taken from her, and one more thing Lisa would have to take care of. She had simply turned off the monitor, not even considering who might find the information later.

* * * * *

Sam saw the look in Angela's eyes and hoped she wasn't thinking what he had tried not to say. He thought of Lisa and John and their flight together. John probably told Lisa his name while they were together. Lisa would have known exactly who he was, but never let on. If she had, John would have told him. Sam thought she had killed John and his sister for revenge because John talked to him. Now, he thought, she probably did it out of spite, simply to hurt Angela. The thought of that suddenly made him concerned for Angela's safety. He now thought there was a possibility that she would be in danger herself. He looked up at the foyer and saw Smith and Saunders watching him. They looked totally engrossed in the story he was telling.

Sam thought that as long as those two were around she would be safe. He would request they not leave her side until Lisa was in custody.

Sam knew the next piece of news would require great delicacy. He looked into her eyes, "I'm really sorry, Angela. She got your father as well."

He could see her eyes suddenly start to glaze over. He knew she understood. "I'm so sorry, Angela. Your father is dead. I think she found out he had been talking to me." He knew he was lying and didn't care. That would be easier for her to take than the truth.

* * * * *

Lisa believed it was destiny. Not only was she able to get on the same flight as John, she even got the seat next to him. They talked during the entire flight and she learned so much about him. She knew what she must do.

Upon arrival, her first task was to book a flight to Mexico. She was sure she had been discreet, but the flight was for insurance, just in case. When everyone had been taken care of, Lisa planned to return and share the details of her exploits with Angela. Lisa thought how gratifying it would be to see Angela's face just before she killed her. She was looking forward to that. Once everyone that had caused her grief was dead, life would be good again.

She decided to spend the night at the hotel she had told her father about. She wanted to stay in the same room that she and Philip had enjoyed. She managed to get the same room as that special night.

* * * * *

Angela now fully realized all that had happened and began crying openly. Sam felt that this demonstration of real emotion was a positive step.

Elaine reached for Angela. Her own eyes were streaming as she pulled her daughter close. She looked back at Sam and could see the remorse on his face. She clearly appreciated his coming and letting them know what had occurred. She was glad to have her daughter back.

Sam began reviewing all the facts. "Lisa was one cold bitch," he thought. He believed the chain of events actually started back when Angela first started going out with Philip. "She had been so mad at her", was the way Angela had put it. Lisa was probably unstable anyway but that single event was the catalyst that pushed her over the edge.

She had probably wanted to be part of the wedding party to get close to Philip, to be part of his life. The set up with the business trip too, was part of her attempts. She probably knew he would go back to her room and they would consummate some kind of relationship. She probably thought the photographs would form some sick wedding album of her own.

She was probably involved with Smythe for the business of marketing the information he had uncovered. It would have been strictly for the money. Her first love would still have been Philip. It was probably the result of her involvement with Smythe and the rejection from Philip that made her consider the extortion.

She did get the money from Philip, Sam thought, but still killed him. He believed she had done that simply to keep him away from Angela. If she couldn't have him, no one would. Maybe she just hated Angela for taking him away and was simply trying to hurt her. That was probably the only reason she killed Simmons too. All just to hurt Angela.

He considered that possibility again. It made sense to him. That was probably her motivation in all of this. She hated Angela desperately and she was eliminating everything in Angela's life that meant anything to her. He was sure of it now. It was all about Angela. The money was simply an added bonus. He knew now that Angela and her mother were both in danger. Lisa wasn't leaving the country at all. She would be coming back here. She would be coming to kill these two, and soon.

* * * * *

Lisa recalled that day at the front desk of the hotel. She was checking out and had heard that bitch talking to the cop. How stupid Diane was, that little lie had been convincing enough but Lisa realized she was running out of time. She needed to act quickly.

Jill answered the door and with gun in hand, Lisa invited herself in. John and Jill were terrified as Lisa stood in front of the fire relaying the tales of her conquests. She remembered the look of disgust on John's face when she told him he was her father. She had been so angry seeing it there. How dare he judge her, after all, she was the result of his genes. He should have been proud of her accomplishments. There was no remorse in her when the gun went off and he slumped onto the couch. The sight of it actually made her smile. When Jill started to run, Lisa remembered giggling and saying, "Don't you dare, Sweetie," and dropped her in her tracks. She remembered her laying face down on the floor. Lisa only hesitated for an instant before shooting her twice more, just to witness the bullets entering her body. The sight of it, and even now the memory of it, made her smile.

As her car rounded the corner, her conscious mind drew her attention to the destination. As she got out of her car, she felt a slight twinge inside. She touched her belly and smiled. She knew it was Philip's and the thought of it made her happy. Soon all the sorrow and grief would be over. She will have made the world safe for her baby - Philip's baby. They will finally be free to live their lives. The gun was in her hand as she approached the front door.

* * * * *

Sam had no sooner completed that thought when he heard a loud bang. It was a split second before he recognized it. A second occurred as he reached into his jacket for his own gun. He looked toward the foyer as Smith and Saunders went down. They had been so engrossed in Sam's tale that they didn't hear the approaching danger. They had not secured the door after Sam's arrival. They had dropped the ball, and paid for it with their lives.

Sam and Lisa faced each other across their outstretched weapons. The two shots had made Angela jump to her feet and she now stood facing the foyer. The third shot echoed through the room and the bullet destined for Sam caught Angela instead. The force of it spun her around and sent her in a heap to the floor. Sam's weapon discharged its cargo a split second later.

His bullet caught Lisa full in the chest. The impact sent Lisa off her feet and back into the foyer. She lay motionless on the floor between the still hulks of Smith and Saunders. Sam muttered under his breath, "Damn." He was cursing himself. His own distraction had allowed Lisa enough time to enter and cause her grief.

He glanced down at Angela. She was obviously in pain but alive. She had stopped the missile that had been intended for him and survived. Dave and Simon were already on their way to Angela. Elaine and Janet were already there. Elaine was in hysterics, "My God. My God. Angela, my God. My sweet baby."

Sam looked back to the foyer and proceeded cautiously towards Lisa's motionless body. Brushing her weapon aside, he knelt beside her and pushed the barrel of his gun hard into her nose. With his free hand he checked her neck for any sign of life. Feeling none, he cursed, "Damn." He had hoped she was still alive. Now they would never know for sure what had been going on in Lisa's mind. Lisa's open eyes displayed absolute terror, as if the last thing they witnessed were the gates of Hell itself.

Smith's body was closest to the front door. He was motionless and Sam reached to check him. No pulse, he was gone. Sam moved on to Saunders, and his neck told the same story - his time was past. Sam shook his head. It had happened so fast, and they were gone. He hadn't really known them but felt a moment of grief just the same.

Returning to the living room, he saw the gathering around Angela. They were frantically trying to offer assistance. Sam returned his gun to its holster as he reached for the phone. He identified himself to the 911 operator and reported the events.

Hanging up, he joined the rest on the floor beside Angela. He saw all the blood soaked hands on her shoulder and gently pushed them aside to get a clear view of her wound. At seeing it, he suspected it wasn't life threatening. It was definitely serious, any gunshot wound is, but she would survive. It made him smile softly, "You are going to be fine, Angela. You hear me? Just relax, the ambulance is on its way." He looked at Dave and Simon. He knew they needed something useful to do. "You guys want to grab some clean towels. We can pack them to control the bleeding."

They both nodded, and got up without saying a word. Sam could tell they were grateful having something to do. His attention went to Elaine who was in terror. He put his hand on her shoulder, "Believe me, Mrs. Michails. She's going to be okay. Understand. She's okay." and nodded at her. She returned the nod but all she knew was her baby was laying on the floor bleeding. Janet sat motionless and crying. She wanted to be doing something, but couldn't move.

Angela's eyes looked distant as they found Sam. She was crying quietly as she focused on his face. "It's my fault. All of it. I did it. They're all dead because of me. I was so selfish. All I cared about was what I wanted. All I cared about was finding my father. I never gave a minutes thought to anyone else. I didn't think about what might happen or who it might affect. Now they are all gone and it's my fault."

The tears she was shedding weren't from the pain of the wound alone but also from the pain of her responsibility in the whole thing. If it hadn't been for her, Lisa would not have done the things she did.

Elaine looked down at her daughter, "Nonsense. Be quiet. It's not your fault. Be quiet. Relax. The ambulance is coming, baby."

The End

A mother holds her child close to her breast and dreams of the possibilities. She will guide, protect, shelter, and nurture her baby until it has grown to make its own way. Choices are made, and their consequences realized. In the end, the light dims and fades. The in-between is the legacy; the memory; the sum; the fuel for judgment.